I DO BELIEVE IN FAERIES

ALSO BY ERIN HAYES

How to be a Mermaid

I'd Rather be a Witch

I Do Believe in Faeries

I'm Not Afraid of Wolves (Coming Summer 2016)

The Harker Trilogy

Damned if I Do

Damned if I Don't (Coming April 2016)

Damned Either Way (Coming June 2016)

Death is but a Dream

Fractured

Jacob Smith is Incredibly Average

Open Hearts

Head Case: A Weird Science Romance (Coming Soon)

Cover art by Lori Parker at Contagious Covers
Edited by Lindsay Galloway at Contagious Edits

SPECIAL THANKS

A special thanks goes to Monica Sofia Igreja, who offered up the name Lucas for a special character.

Thank you so much. I can't wait for you to read it here.

For Chris, who put a spell on me ten years ago.

CHAPTER 1

"ABBY, ARE YOU COMING?"

I looked up from the Pinterest boards on my iPhone and pulled out my earbuds. "What?"

My sister Jordyn stood in the doorway of the kitchen, her purse in one hand and the keys to Mom's Honda Accord in the other.

"I'm heading up to Jacksonville to see Alaina," she explained, spinning the keys absently.

I narrowed my eyes, trying to remember who Alaina was. Nothing came to mind.

Jordyn sighed and flipped her too-cool pink hair over her shoulder. "Alaina Hoover? One of my mermaid friends?"

Ah, now I remembered. Jordyn used to be a professional mermaid, and Alaina was one of her teammates whose troupe trained in Jacksonville.

"She's back in town?" I asked. "I thought the mermaids were still on tour."

Jordyn shrugged. "Well, Neptune and Christine are still on tour with the other mermaids—I guess they were able to find replacements in Los Angeles." She waved her hand dismissively. "Anyways, Alaina's back because she's expecting her baby."

I made a face. "Ew, babies," I joked.

Jordyn rolled her eyes, disagreeing with my weird sense of humor. Sometimes I wondered if we were really sisters or if I was adopted. It would sure make sense.

Jordyn was happy for the first time in a long time. I suspected it was more than coming back home after being gone for three years—she had a boyfriend here to make her feel special. Meanwhile, me… Well, I wasn't feeling special.

"I already told you all of this earlier and you said sure," Jordyn groaned. "Now I'm starting to think you were listening to One Direction again.

"Probably." I was always listening to One Direction.

"Come on," she pleaded. "You need to get out of the house and stop looking at hot guys on Instagram."

My cheeks blushed. "I'm looking at prom dresses *on Pinterest*, thank you very much!"

She smirked. "It'll be good for you."

"Why do you want me to come along? She's *your* friend."

"Because Mom thinks you've been moping around the house, and I want you to meet some of my mermaid friends. Now, are you coming?" With a quick swipe of her hand, she used magick to hit the home button on my iPhone from afar, closing my app.

"Hey!" There was more anger in my voice than I

should have had, but it wasn't fair that Jordyn was able to use magick to tease me when I couldn't reciprocate.

"Come *on*, Abby, stop being such a teenager." Strong words from someone who was just barely outside of being one herself. I was seventeen, so I was practically in my twenties, right?

I groaned as I got up from my spot at the kitchen island. "You owe me."

Jordyn gave me a half-lazy smile and smacked me in the butt as I headed out the door.

Oh yeah, it was *such* a good thing having my big sister back in my life.

***

"OH MY *GOD*, ALAINA! YOU'VE GOTTEN SO BIG!"

I watched as my sister hugged someone who was heavily preggers. Alaina was pretty, I decided, with dark hair and olive skin that accentuated her green eyes. A little older than Jordyn, she had a worldliness to her that my sister and I could never hope to pull off.

"Look at you, Jordyn!" Alaina exclaimed. "You look wonderful!"

Oh great, this is a reunion where both of the gorgeous girls tell each other how gorgeous they are.

Jealousy nagged at the back of my head. It's not that I wasn't pretty myself—I was *decent* and I was popular at school, not that being popular made life easy. It's just, in my world of magick, I had so many things going against me, like being unable to perform magick. Unlike the rest of my family.

I kept my smile frozen on my face as they continued talking, waiting for the moment when one of them remembered me.

Why am I here again?

I could have been picking out my shoes for my prom. Granted, it was a month and a half from now, but I could never start too early. I wanted to impress Christian Meyer, since I doubted he knew I was alive.

Jordyn looked back at me and hooked her arm through mine

"This is my kid sister, Abby," Jordyn said, bringing me forward.

She called me her *"kid sister"*. I could die.

A brilliant smile spread across Alaina's face as she saw me. "Hi, I'm Alaina," she said, holding her hand out for a shake. I took it awkwardly. "You have no idea how much Jordyn has talked about you over the years. I can't believe we haven't gotten together like this the entire time."

Jordyn and I exchanged glances.

"Oh, you know," Jordyn said. "The timing just never worked out."

That was mostly true. Mom and I visited Jordyn when she lived in Jacksonville, but we never met her coworkers because we were always in a hurry to get back to our town of Centerburg, Florida, to protect everyone from a borderline psycho killer. Yeah, magick really messed with our lives for a while.

And the absence of it will continue to mess up my life.

Alaina beamed at me. "A sister to Jordyn is a sister to me," she said. "It's nice to finally meet you."

"Yeah," I said. "Sure."

We had lunch at this beachside restaurant in Jacksonville that had really good burgers and fried fish. I was here a long time ago with Mom and Jordyn, and it was nice to see that the place hadn't changed one bit.

Here, Jordyn was in her element. I could tell that she loved the city and the life she made here. I wondered how she felt moving back to little ol' Centerburg—because all I wanted to do was to leave it—but I think being close to Mom and Luke was the icing on her proverbial cake.

Meanwhile, Alaina was talking about her plans for her baby, how she was setting up a nursery with her boyfriend in downtown Jacksonville. She was on leave from the mermaid troupe, but I got the feeling that she was going to move on to another career to be there for her small family. She was asking Jordyn a lot about how she liked nursing school, so maybe she was considering that.

My ears were itching to hear more One Direction as I listened to them talk. I wanted to slip back inside my iPhone and fall in love with Harry Styles all over again.

"Tell me about yourself, Abby," Alaina said, turning her green eyes on me.

I blinked, taken aback. "Me?"

"I'm sure it was fun growing up with Jordyn as a big sister," Alaina said, before she bit into her burger.

Oh, you have no idea.

"Jordyn was the favorite," I said with a half-hearted laugh.

Across the table, Jordyn frowned and put down the French fry she was about to eat. "No I wasn't."

"Oh yeah you were," I countered, rolling my eyes. "You were always the talented one."

Jordyn narrowed her eyes as she glared at me. Alaina blinked, unsure of where this conversation was going.

To be honest, I didn't know where it was going either. I didn't know why I was being so surly right now, but I think it's because I just wanted to be left alone at the house on a Saturday. Certain things about my life were irritating me. Mainly the fact that Jordyn could screw things up, but life always worked out for her. And here I was, working my butt off and the needle never seemed to tip.

Maybe I was acting like a spoiled brat, but I didn't care. It was a long time coming.

Alaina dabbed her mouth with her napkin, sensing my annoyance. "I've gotta go to the bathroom," she said, pushing herself to her feet. "I'll be right back, okay?"

As she headed towards the bathroom, Jordyn leaned into the table. "What was that?" she hissed.

"What?"

"*That!*"

I crossed my arms. "It's just not fair."

"Is this about magick again?"

Ashamed, I didn't meet her eyes.

Jordyn sighed. "Look, Abby." She reached across the table and took my hand in hers. "We're working on your *Book of Shadows*. We're practicing. Aunt Margaret and Mom are doing everything possible to get you in touch with nature. It will come to you, I promise."

"I'm almost eighteen years old," I said, "and I've never been able to do magick. It's not just suddenly going to pop out of nowhere, like a pimple."

Jordyn's lips quirked into a half smile at my analogy.

"It's not funny, Jordyn." Even though it was.

She squeezed my hand. "We'll find a way."

I wished I could believe her, but since I was a little girl, I had been trying so damn hard to be a witch like her. There had been nothing to give me any sort of hope.

It sucked the big one.

"Sorry about that."

We both looked up to see Alaina standing there, sheepish. "I have to pee every five minutes because of this baby," she explained apologetically.

"That's all right," Jordyn said, sitting back as she watched me pointedly. "Abby and I were just talking."

"Yeah," I said, putting a fry to my lips. "Just talking."

I would have given anything to magick myself away to my room back at the house so I could cry, but you have to have magick to do that.

And I certainly didn't.

I finished my lunch in silence, sulking into my fish and chips while Jordyn and Alaina talked about everything from porpoises to boyfriends. All of which I couldn't relate to.

What did surprise me though, was when we got up to leave after a few hours, Alaina wrapped me up in a tight hug.

"So nice meeting you!" she said. "And I understand where you're coming from, Abby. So if you need anything, just let me know, okay?"

Her gesture touched me, but there was one thing I knew for certain.

She didn't understand anything.

***

"I thought every bit of magick that you used had to be paid back in thrice," I said, trying to shrink down into my seat as Jordyn drove back to Centerburg. Jordyn was driving like a maniac, using magick to make the stoplights go green and creating space in the lane next to us to get around a truck. Had I known she was going to drive like this, I would have *never* gone with her to meet Alaina.

She glanced at me and grinned. "This is little magick. It probably just amounts to me losing a few hairs on my head."

Now I knew why Jordyn sheds like a fluffy dog. At the rate she's going, she'll be bald in a week.

"Ew," I said. "And you and I share the same shower."

"We're making great time getting home," she said.

"Stop showing off."

"I just want to be there for dinner with Mom and Aunt Margaret."

"And Luke's coming over, too," I snickered, bringing up her boyfriend.

"Well, there's always that," Jordyn added sheepishly.

Everything always worked out for Jordyn. She had an awesome boyfriend growing up. She still had an awesome boyfriend now. She still had magick. She was still the gifted Murphy daughter.

The thought made me sink further into my seat.

Luke's cop car was already in the driveway when we pulled up to our house, meaning that he had come straight from work. Jordyn's face lit up and I couldn't help but frown. It wasn't that I didn't like Luke. He was mostly okay. I was just sick of being the average little sister.

"Are you okay?"

I looked back at my sister and then pasted on a fake smile.

"Peachy keen."

Yeah right.

CHAPTER 2

MOM MIGHT HAVE KNOWN HOW TO PULL A rabbit out of a hat using magick, but she never could get the whole cooking thing down. After forcing down her Pork Casserole surprise, we all sat back quietly, still picking the dried bits of pork out of our teeth.

"How was it?" Mom asked hopefully, as she began collecting our plates to do the dishes. To fill the silence, Jordyn got up and helped her, all the while looking at me for an answer.

Luckily, Aunt Margaret saved us. "It was filling," the older woman said. Really, that was the only thing she could say about it. "Very filling."

Mom sighed. "Another failure, huh?"

"Yep," Aunt Margaret said honestly. Our great-aunt never sugarcoated anything. I wished she had made her chocolate cake. At least that would have been something with flavor.

"I thought it was good," Luke offered, politely wiping his mouth with his napkin. The goody two-shoes, although he blushed as he said it.

I snickered, and Aunt Margaret frowned at me in

response.

"Maybe it needs more frozen peas," Mom muttered to herself as she picked up my plate.

Jordyn glared at me as she followed Mom into the kitchen, something akin to accusation in her eyes.

What did I do?

For all I knew, she and Aunt Margaret magicked something in there to make it taste palatable. I didn't know if that was possible, but it would make sense. Luke and I would have had to choke down the food with our normal-person throats.

I sighed exasperatedly and pushed my seat back. It was time to head back upstairs and listen to Taylor Swift while I looked at prom dresses. I wanted to lose myself in stuff that I had some control over.

"Where are you going?" Aunt Margaret asked, raising a suspicious eyebrow. Nothing gets past her. Imagine growing up with a woman who could look you in the eye and tell exactly what you were thinking.

It kinda sucked.

"To do homework," I lied. "Maybe go to Starbucks so I can get some privacy." That last part held truth. I wanted to get out of house so I could be by myself.

My great-aunt didn't buy it. I could tell because her forehead creased ever so slightly.

"I have a test tomorrow," I added, throwing more fuel into the fire. *A test on Monday. Sure.*

Aunt Margaret nodded and waved me away. That was

as much of an answer as I was going to get.

"Have a good night, Luke," I told my sister's boyfriend. I didn't know if he was staying longer, or if she was going to go over to his place, and frankly, I didn't want to know. Still though, I wanted to be nice to him. He was a good guy.

"See you, Abby," he called after me, as I trudged up the steps.

My family's cat, Sadie, sat at the top of the landing, giving me the stink eye. "Not you too," I sighed. Even the cat was judgmental.

She continued to glare at me as I stepped around her. Darn thing refused to move, just like any cat would. I sighed as I finally made it to my room.

I did have homework, but there was no way I was going to be able to focus on that right now. I looked at my phone, debated on listening to music while hiding in my room.

Then I heard Jordyn's laughter rise up from downstairs.

No, I really needed to get out of here. Where, I didn't care.

I grabbed my jacket and my keys, and as I did, my *Book of Shadows* fell onto the floor. Jordyn had been helping me work on the *Book*, but I grew frustrated and put the *Book* away. The binder had just been sitting in the corner for a while now, waiting to be used again. I'd never be able to use it properly.

I frowned.

No.

I refused to let something like not having the gift get in the way of me practicing magick. I'm a Murphy, dammit. My family has been persecuted for generations for being witches, and I wasn't going to be the one exception.

If I was going to suffer for their sins, I was going to learn to sin myself.

It never bothered me before Jordyn got back, but after I saw how differently Aunt Margaret treated her, and how much easier life is for her, I made a vow. I was going to learn magick..

Magick is 95% willpower, right? Well, I had 100%.

I grabbed the binder and tucked it under my arm. I put my phone in my backpack and left my room, sidestepping Sadie again, who hadn't moved from her spot. The cat didn't even bother to look at me as I passed her. Her blasé attitude was confirmation that I needed to get out as I took the stairs two at a time.

"I'll be back!" I called, as I opened the door, meaning to leave without further interruptions. Unfortunately, the last person I wanted to see popped her head around the corner and I inwardly groaned.

I shouldn't have said anything.

"Where are you going?" Jordyn asked. She crossed her arms as she leaned against the door jamb.

"Out."

Her eyes flicked to the *Book of Shadows* that I held in

the crook of my arm. "Oh!" she said, surprised. "Are you going to practice magick?"

"N—no!"

"Want me to come with you?"

"No," I repeated, backing up.

Jordyn saw me retreating and stopped. "Are you okay?" she asked. "You've been acting so *strange* lately."

"I'm fine," I said a little too quickly.

"Is it because of a boy?"

Her question was so stupid, I almost laughed. Her perception of me was all wrong, and it actually hurt. "No, Jordyn, it's not because of a boy."

"Then why?"

My bottom lip trembled. Should I tell her? She was trying to help, sure, but at the same time, she was a lot of the reason why I was "acting strange".

"You can tell me," she assured me, and she clapped me on the upper arm.

The touch made me explode from within.

"You just don't get it, do you?" Now she was the one who stepped back, astonished by my outburst, but I was nowhere near done. "You screw up—*royally*—and tear apart our family. Then you come back after three years, and it's as though everything is all right. Well, guess what? It's not! You've had so many second chances. And me…I'm not even a real witch. I never even had a first chance."

Jordyn's eyes turned hard at that last part. "I told you, we're working on that."

"It's not just about that!" I threw up my free hand in anger and rather than say anything else, I opened the door and walked out to my car.

Of course Jordyn followed me. "What is it then?" she demanded.

"Nothing," I said, unlocking the door and throwing my backpack and *Book of Shadows* in the backseat.

Jordyn narrowed her eyes at me casually tossing my *Book* around. "You need to treat your *Book of Shadows* better than that."

"It's just a binder right now. I'm not a witch, remember? Not like you."

"Abby…"

"You know what the worst part is?" I asked, opening the driver's side door. "I'm stuck with the realization that Dad left us because you and Mom are witches. But what about me, huh? I'm not even a witch. I don't deserve this. I don't deserve to be treated differently because of that."

Ouch. Even as I said it, I knew I'd gone too far.

Jordyn's face twisted into anger. She probably would have slapped me if she was closer, and I was surprised that she didn't use magick to do just that. I used her shock to get into the car, close the door, turn it on, and drive away, leaving her there.

And as I drove off, I couldn't help but cry.

CHAPTER 3

I DIDN'T GO TO STARBUCKS OR TO THE LIBRARY to work on stuff for school. Instead, I followed through on my plans to practice magick and see if there was an inkling—*anything*—resembling a witch within me.

I parked outside of Shady Point, a forest on the outskirts of town. After a few nightmarish events that have happened here, I should have been scared of the place.

But I wasn't.

Not tonight, because I was feeling fiery and defiant. I wanted to be alone, and the only place where I could be alone was Shady Point. Plus, it was the last place where Jordyn would look for me.

If she was even looking for me after I exploded in the driveway.

I stepped out of the car and took a deep breath, smelling the sweet scent of pine and damp earth. Maybe if I breathed it in enough, it would help me connect with nature. Jordyn and Mom used earth-based magick, so I imagined, hypothetically, that's what I'd be able to use too.

I shook my head trying to clear it of the nagging doubt that threatened to derail me. I grabbed my *Book* and my backpack and took off for the deep part of the woods.

After spending my entire life in Centerburg, I was pretty familiar with Shady Point in the daytime. We had Easter Egg hunts here when we were little. Many of my class trips were to Shady Point to do some experiments (although I think many of the experiments were boys and girls kissing when they were out of sight of the teachers). I'd gone here with Jordyn to play hide-and-seek when we were very young.

I missed those days. when the world seemed fair and just. Yet, after everything that happened with Jordyn's old boyfriend, and our psychotic neighbor Mr. Samson, the woods and my memories were tainted. I'd seen how far humans would go to hurt each other.

Anyhow, I should have been more scared, but there was one thing about being determined to use magick: I was also determined to be dumb.

After wandering for a bit, I finally spotted it. There was a big oak tree about a fifteen minute walk from the parking lot. I had no idea how old it was, only that it must have been ancient because it was wider than my car, and the bark was almost a brownish gray from age. The thick roots of the oak tree wound into the ground like a complex network of pipes, and it towered over the other trees around it, throwing them into deeper shadow.

The tree was beautiful in an unsettling, soul-touching way. I'd found it on one of those hide-and-seek excursions when we were little. Being three years older than me, Jordyn was always better at it than me and could always find me (she cheated sometimes with magick). When I stumbled on this big tree, I hid in it for hours until Mom panicked and went out to go find me. After that day, Jordyn and I always made it a point to come out here and climb this tree.

Of course, that was years ago, and we hadn't been back to the old oak tree since.

As I walked up to it, I picked up a fallen leaf that dwarfed the palm of my hand. And I saw that a circle of mushrooms had sprouted up in the tree's shade.

This felt like a sacred, ancient place.

"Hey there, big guy. Remember me?" I said to the oak tree. "I'm here to see if I can be a witch."

I don't know why I was talking to it, only that there was no one else around, and I felt like saying something to it. Maybe it was because I would have given anything to have someone there with me.

Someone who understood me.

No one understands you, Abby.

I hated those bad thoughts.

The moon was a crescent, throwing just enough light into the glade for me to read. I took a seat on one of the roots and opened up my Book. I stifled a sigh as I ran my hand down the first page.

"This the Book of Shadows of Abigail Murphy, an Earth-based witch."

Yeah, right, I thought, reading that last part.

I needed to stop those kinds of thoughts. Starting

now.

As a first step in the right direction, I pulled out my candles, ready to cast a circle so I could perform magick. My hand briefly touched my phone, and I glanced at the screen. There were five text messages and a missed call from Jordyn. I really didn't want to deal with her right now. Mainly because I had no idea what I would say. So instead, I put it away and stood up.

"All right," I said to the tree and whatever magick was around me to listen. I rolled up my figurative sleeves. "Let's get started."

***

"DAMMIT! WHY AREN'T YOU WORKING RIGHT?!"

I slammed my *Book* shut and threw it away from. I heard it thump somewhere in the darkness, but I didn't care. Tears stung my eyes, and I heaved heavy sobs.

Nothing was working.

I had tried *everything*. I'd tried casting a circle. Nothing happened. I'd tried some divinations. Again, nothing happened. I'd even tried making a charm, and it was just a worthless pinch of sage and rosemary.

Why was I like this? Why couldn't I have been a witch like Jordyn? That's all I wanted in the world. To be accepted by my family. To be an earth-based witch. At home, I wasn't weird enough. At school, I was too weird because I came from a family of witches.

I was the outcast everywhere.

Why, I wish, I wish that I could—

"I wouldn't do that if I were you, Tinkerbell."

I froze, my sob stuck halfway in my throat. Frantic, I looked around, trying to find the source of that voice. Who would be talking to a seventeen-year-old girl in the middle of the woods at night? And should I start running?

"Who's there?" I demanded, my voice wavering from fright.

"Me," the voice said. It seemed to be everywhere around me, so I couldn't track where it was coming from.

"Where are you?" I asked.

"Here." It came from right beside me, and I jumped. "No, wait, here." That time, it was in the boughs of the tree.

I may not be a witch who could conjure up some fire, but I could conjure up some light. I grabbed my phone and found the flashlight app. I swept the beam of light around the base of the tree, trying to find the source of the voice.

"Show yourself!" I called out, like I was trying to be some sort of superhero.

There was silence for a beat, then came:

"Well, if you insist then, Tinkerbell."

A loud *pop* sounded.

I screamed as a face appeared in front of me, and I fell backwards, landing hard on my rump. I didn't even get that good of a look at the face before I screamed, but as I looked up, I now saw a...*guy*...standing before me.

And not just any guy either. He looked like he was in his early twenties—at least it seemed like it because there was something youthful about him, yet at the same time he seemed ancient. He had a shock of red hair, and while I don't normally go for gingers, he was *gorgeous*. Like, Harry Styles and Chris Evans had a baby with red hair and it was this guy.

He looked very unimpressed at my reaction. "You did insist on me showing myself," he told me.

"I didn't mean like that!"

He quirked a smile, a mischievous one that reminded me of an imp, and offered me his hand. I didn't need help getting up so I batted him away. He looked hurt.

"You offer to help a dame, and still she fights you," he sighed.

"I'm fine," I gritted. "Who are you? What are you doing out in the woods?"

"Well, I could ask the same of you, Tinkerbell," he countered.

Good point.

"Why're you calling me Tinkerbell?"

He shrugged. "Seemed appropriate."

I slowly got to my feet, rubbing my backside with my free hand. "I was just out here…"

"About to make a wish inside a Faerie Ring, and you really shouldn't do that," he chided. He even clucked his tongue to my irritation.

"What's a Faerie Ring?" I asked.

He groaned and scratched at his head (and yes, I paid way too much attention to the way his bicep bulged when his arm bent like that). "A Faerie Ring? You know, a circle of mushrooms?"

I looked down at the mushrooms around me, burrowed into the ground. "So?"

He snickered and shook his head. "That's where faeries dance, idiot."

It took a moment for that to sink in, but once it did, I burst out laughing. I mean, seriously, faeries? I know I come from a family of witches, and that magick is all around us. I know that there are a lot of things that we could never explain.

But faeries? Like the Tooth Fairy? He needed to get real. No wonder he was calling me "Tinkerbell". He was a nutcase.

"You don't believe me," he intoned at my laughing.

"No, I really don't," I said, letting my laughter subside. "Because that's stupid."

He raised an eyebrow. "You shouldn't make fun of faeries," he said, his voice dangerous. "Although I think it's their influence that's making *you* stupid."

"That's a really bad comeback."

But once again, his expression had turned so serious, that I giggled even more. Maybe it was the stress or maybe it was because I was being mean, but either way, it felt good to laugh.

"Let me guess, you're a faerie?" I asked.

His severe expression answered that yes, yes he was a faerie. Or at least he thought he was.

"Where are your wings then?" I teased. Adrenaline and fear propelled me to move forward and look behind him to see if there were anything resembling wings. He stepped backwards, frowning unhappily.

"Not all faeries have wings, dingus."

"Oh, right. So what kind of faerie are you, then?"

He gave me a hard look, bristled, then said, "I'm Robin Goodfellow. Otherwise known as Puck," he added with a touch of pride.

"Puck?" That set my brain working and I stepped back. "As in *A Midnight's Summer Dream*?" I was supposed to read that book for English class last year, but I picked up the summaries online. Though, admittedly, I didn't even read them.

He rolled his eyes. "It's *A Midsummer Night's Dream*," he corrected. "Everyone knows me from that, but yes, that's me."

"Uh huh. Right."

This totally hot guy was telling me that he was both a faerie and character from a William Shakespeare play. I should have been running for the hills, back to my car. Crazy always followed my family around, but this was the first time it ever talked to me. In the dark woods. Alone.

Yet something compelled me to stay. It might have been because he was hot. Whatever it was, I wanted to keep talking to him. "Okay, Robin Goodfellow, what were you saying about not making a wish in a Faerie Ring?" I ventured, crossing my arms.

He groaned again and threw up his hands. "You mortals always ask too many questions. I should have just let you make the wish."

"Then what would have happened?"

"It would have come true."

His vibrant green eyes met mine, and I found myself holding my breath. "I can't tell when you're joking and when you're serious," I said softly, the bravado gone from my voice.

He cast his eyes away from me, as if he knew the effect he was having on me. "I'm being as serious as death."

I opened my mouth to ask what he meant by that, but I was cut off by something that sounded like the wind rustling through the trees. Only it wasn't the wind.

"Make the wish, Abby..."

It was almost indistinct, and it sounded like little children whispering secrets to each other, both boys and girls. Then I realized that a tense quiet had fallen in the woods.

"What was that?" I asked, spinning around to look around us.

Robin looked behind him, then his eyes went skyward as he groaned again. "Just pixies. Don't pay them any mind."

"Pixies?"

At my question, the wind picked up again, blowing

leaves in my direction. *"We're real, Abby. Just make the wish…"*

"You're…serious," I said, as it finally dawned on me that all of what he said might have been true, as crazy as it sounded.

Robin stuffed his hands in his pockets and looked at me. "I tried warning you." That dangerous tone was back in his voice, and I wasn't sure where it was coming from.

"I'm not sure that counts as a warning, because if these pixies can make any wish come true…"

I know what I'd wish for.

In a heartbeat.

It was selfish, yes. I could have wished for world peace. Or for my family to never have to worry about bills again. I could wish for a whole bunch of things, but one wish stood out in my mind, clear as day. A wish that I'd wanted for as long as I could remember.

"Make the wish, Abby… Make the wish!" The wind picked up again, fluttering my hair as I met his intense gaze again. He was pleading with me, first with his eyes, then his voice. And I didn't know why.

"Don't, Abby."

I wondered how they all knew my name. If it was really magick, then it made sense, in a weird sort of way. If I remembered correctly, faeries are tricksters, but this put my ultimate dream so close, I could taste it.

My heart pounded in my chest.

"I wish I had magick."

I watched as Robin's face fell at my words. But why?

I just made a wish, and—

The woods around us came to life with chattering from the pixies, building in crescendo as they celebrated.

"Magick! Magick! She wishes for magick!"

Their elation was contagious, and I couldn't help but smile, which was quickly dashed when I saw Robin turn away from me and take a step into the wood.

"What's wrong?"

He glanced back at me, fury in his eyes. "Any wish requires a sacrifice."

"A sacrifice!" The pixies chittered around us. *"The wish requires a sacrifice!"*

Just like magick.

That didn't sound good. I shivered, feeling the icy hand of dread take hold of my stomach and twisting. A sacrifice? No, that's not right. That's not what I wanted at all.

I felt the press of little bodies scuttling around me, things that I couldn't see, but I could certainly feel. "Hey!" I cried as something tugged hard on my hair.

"A sacrifice!" the pixies cried, more insistent. *"A sacrifice!"*

Their voices filled the inside of my head. I cried out and covered my ears with my hands, even though I could feel their little bodies scrabbling along my skin. That didn't stop the phrase echoing inside my head, making the world spin around me. I fell to my knees as I tried blocking them out, but it didn't help at all.

"A sacrifice! A sacrifice!"

Images began flashing through my mind, one after the other like a Powerpoint presentation. Of my family, of Jordyn leaving us, of my school, of my most embarrassing moment.

Everything. Even things I'd forgotten, like Dad's face peering down at me when I was swaddled in a crib. Playing with Jordyn and Zach and Luke in our backyards.

Then Alaina appeared in my mind's eye, smiling at me.

"Tell me about yourself, Abby," she had said.

Then, my memory's eye sidled down and I looked at her swollen belly and the baby that's growing inside.

"If you need anything, just let me know, okay?" I remembered Alaina telling me.

No, no, no.

"That will do," the voices said.

"Wait, what?" I shouted.

"The sacrifice has been made."

I looked around wildly, as the tiny little hands in my hair, and on my body, disappeared. With a *whoosh*, the wind in the woods died, leaving me alone with Robin, who was watching me curiously.

Self-conscious, I swatted away at the air. "What happened?"

"I tried warning you, Tinkerbell," he said softly.

"*What* happened?!"

He just shook his head.

Frantic, I ran to him, reaching out with my hands to take him by the scruff of his shirt. Only, when my fingers connected with his shirt, they found nothing.

He had disappeared right before my eyes.

"Oh my god."

He really was a faerie. And those really were pixies.

I collapsed to my knees, feeling my pulse race. It felt like my mind moved too slowly to fully process these events. None of it made sense.

Maybe it's all just a dream.

Maybe...

My phone rang, which was weird, because I distinctly remembered that it had been on silent. I grabbed at it, glad for some semblance of reality.

"Hello?"

"Abby!" Mom's voice came through the speaker so loudly, I had to hold it away from my ear. I winced. "Abby, where the hell are you? I've been trying to call you!"

"I..."

"It's one in the morning, young lady!"

I blinked. One in the morning? But that means I'd been here for something like five hours, and surely... surely...

I glanced at my phone's clock. 1:07am. Oh my god, I really had been here for that long.

"Time slipped away from me," I told Mom honestly. After all, I wasn't lying. I started packing up my things. I wanted to get out of here as soon as possible.

"That's no excuse, and you know that."

Oh, Mom, if you only knew what had happened to me.

For a second, I thought about telling her. She was a witch, she understood magick and everything that came with it. Then I struck that thought from my mind—after all, I'd been talking with faeries. And talking about faeries was crazy.

No, this was something that I should keep to myself. I could just imagine Aunt Margaret's expression as I relayed that story to them. Aunt Margaret made some great unimpressed facial expressions. Almost as good as Robin's unimpressed look, and the very memory of that made my insides squirm.

So I didn't tell her.

Instead, she launched into a long lecture about how she trusted me, and if I was going to stay out past my curfew, she was going to put me on a tighter leash. After all, when her other daughter was my age, she had brought her boyfriend back from the dead.

In fact, her lecture lasted my entire walk back to my car, ending when I unlocked the door.

"I'll be home in fifteen minutes," I told her.

"Where are you where it would take fifteen minutes?" Mom demanded, her voice raising an octave.

"IHOP," I lied. It was the first thing that popped into my head, and I didn't know of any other place that was open this late.

Thankfully, Mom bought it.

"You come home. Right. Now." She hung up without saying good-bye.

I tossed my phone into my passenger seat and drummed my hands on the steering wheel for a second, calming my adrenaline after everything that had happened.

I didn't *feel* any different, which made me question if I had really encountered Robin Goodfellow and a bunch of pixies. Maybe they didn't grant my wish. Or maybe, which was the more likely explanation, I had dreamed the whole thing. Maybe I was hallucinating. After all, I could have accidentally ingested one of the mushrooms while trying out my spells. Unlikely, though.

I hoped it was real.

It would certainly be a shame if Robin wasn't real. Because I think I kinda liked him.

CHAPTER 4

LO AND BEHOLD, I COULDN'T SLEEP.

It was sometime after three in the morning, and I kept tossing and turning. I don't think it was from the hard talk that Mom gave me when I got home—even though I did get an earful and more. Every time I closed my eyes, I kept thinking of green-eyed faerie men and pixies crawling all over my skin.

One mental image was hot. And the other totally was not.

I itched all over, like I had pins and needles stabbing me. I wanted to crawl out of my shell of a human body and be something else. What, I didn't know. It was sure uncomfortable, though.

I harrumphed as I flipped to my back and looked up at the ceiling. I still had these little glow-in-the-dark stars that I'd put up there when I was six years old. Jordyn had helped me, and we tried putting each five-pointed star into constellations. So many nights, I had looked up at this ceiling and memorized every little detail.

I was a teenager with chronic insomnia. Tonight, though, it was really bad, much worse than usual. Questions swirled in my brain, and I tried connecting the dots like they were far-flung parts of a constellation. Nothing made sense. And everything seemed like a far off dream.

Did I have magick? Did those pixies really grant me a wish? I was itching to try it out but there was no way I was going to be able to get out of the house tonight, not after mom already busted me on curfew.

What sacrifice might they have taken in return? The last thing I remembered was seeing Alaina before they accepted it.

I rolled onto my side, facing the doorway. The night light had burned out a long time ago but I could see the outline of it. It was in the shape of a crescent moon, purposefully picked out to match my ceiling-sky.

It suddenly irritated me that it had died. My room was dark and even the glow-in-the-dark stars on the ceiling had winked out due to there not being any light in my room.

I focused on the nightlight, concentrating on each and every detail. I could almost imagine my consciousness running up and down the filament in the bulb, imbuing it with a piece of myself to breathe some life back into it.

But that was crazy, because I had no magick within me.

Then…*then*…

It started as a small glow, so small that I thought it was a trick of my eyes. Then it grew stronger, a bluish light that threw shadows across my room. I blinked in confusion. Was I doing that? Or was it just suddenly coming back to life in a wacky, strange coincidence?

Whatever caused it, there was definitely a light emanating from that light bulb, shuddering in its socket. The light danced off the wall with the movement.

"Abby!"

Jordyn threw open the door to my bedroom. That very action disoriented me enough that I stopped concentrating on the nightlight, throwing my room back into instant darkness.

My first thought was a panicked, *Oh, crap, she saw what I was doing!* The second thought was, *I guess she stayed here tonight."*

And then I saw her tears.

I sat bolt upright in bed. The elation from possibly doing any sort of magick came crashing down, concern for my sister surging to the surface.

"What's wrong?" I asked.

Jordyn wrung her hands as she came over to my bed. She plopped down next to me and put her head in her hands, sobs wracking her body.

"What happened?" I asked.

Did her ex-boyfriend Zach come back from the dead a second time? Or did something else…?

"It's Alaina…" Jordyn managed between her tears. "…her—her baby…"

My body went rigid as I remembered the last image that came through my mind before the pixies claimed that their "sacrifice" had been made.

"What about her baby?" I asked.

Jordyn blinked at me. "She's at the hospital. Her baby…It's…*missing*."

***

"HOW THE HELL DOES AN UNBORN BABY GO missing?" Luke asked as he drove both of us to the Jacksonville hospital. Thank god for good boyfriends. Jordyn was in no condition to drive and I was too freaked out to attempt it. She immediately wanted to go to the hospital and console her friend. I never had as much respect for her as I did in that moment.

"I—I don't know what happened!" Jordyn sobbed.

She sat in the passenger seat, dabbing at her eyes with a tissue. I didn't realize until this moment how close my sister was to all of her mermaid friends. They were like their own little family. They'd do anything for each other. I wondered if I would ever experience that kind of sisterly love from any of my friends.

"Tell him what happened," I prompted from my seat in the back of Luke's Prius. She had already told me, but I needed to hear it again. Maybe it would make more sense and keep me from freaking out if I heard it a second time.

"Alaina woke up with bad stomach pains. She thought she was having early contractions, so she went to the emergency room. And when the doctor checked her out…there wasn't a baby. Like she never was pregnant in the first place."

"How?" Luke asked again.

"I don't know. The baby is just…*gone*…apparently." Jordyn chewed at her bottom lip. "She fainted when she heard the news. Her boyfriend is there right now. Oh god, I don't know what to do."

She combed her hands through her pink hair. I wished there was something that I could do, anything that would help. If I truly had magick…

Alaina's baby was the sacrifice so that you could wish for magick.

The ugly thought reared its head in my mind, and I blinked furiously to stop the tears from falling.

I was responsible for this.

I'd just traded Alaina's baby for magick.

"Stop the car!" I demanded.

"What?" Luke asked.

"Stop the car, now!"

I didn't even wait for Luke to come to a full stop before opening the door. I bent over the side and threw up the remains of the pork casserole that Mom had made for dinner onto the side of the road.

***

AS WE HEADED DOWN THE HALLWAY OF THE hospital, a tired-looking man around Luke's age came out of a room to meet us.

"James!" Jordyn said, rushing to give him a hug.

"Oh, thank god you're here," the guy murmured. He looked like he was barely keeping it together as he wrapped his arms around my older sister. I figured he was Alaina's boyfriend.

What do you say in this situation?

"Where is she?" Jordyn asked.

James looked stricken for a moment before sighing. "She's…here…" As he spoke, he opened the door to the room he just came out of. I looked around and saw Alaina laying in a hospital bed. Contrary to the bubbly, pretty girl that I had seen at lunch yesterday, she looked small and frail, her skin a ghastly shade of gray.

I swallowed back more bile as it formed in my throat.

"I don't want to disturb her," James whispered. "She's been having nightmares and they had to sedate her because she was thrashing around so badly. I just…" His face crumpled as he collapsed back into a chair. Jordyn took a seat next to him and rubbed his back, murmuring some things that I couldn't hear.

Why did I come? I couldn't do anything; I would just get in the way. Like usual.

"I need some air," I rasped to Luke. My throat burned from where I had heaved up the contents of my stomach.

He nodded, not really listening to me. His eyes kept flicking between his girlfriend and the still form of Alaina in her room.

I took that moment to back away. I turned tail and

ran. I had no idea where I was going, I just needed to get out and breathe in something that wasn't their despair.

Possibly caused by me. Probably.

I wound through corridor after corridor. Every hallway looked the same. White glossy floors and locked doors. Somehow, I ended up on the ground floor of the hospital and I pushed open the doors to the outside. I found myself in some sort of nature preserve. Like a small park in the middle of the hospital complex, it must have been a place where the administration thought they could make patients forget that they were sick.

It didn't make me feel any better.

I took a seat on a wooden bench. I tried inhaling big, deep breaths, but my lungs didn't seem to want to fill with air.

I'd caused their pain.

And for what? So I could turn on the night light in my room? I didn't care what other magick I had—if I had any more magick to show.

I would have given anything to have Alaina's baby back.

"I tried to warn you," a familiar voice said, breaking through my thoughts.

I shrieked and jumped, seeing that the red-haired faerie boy had appeared on the bench next to me. Anger quickly overtook surprise, and I sprang to my feet.

"You!" I roared. "You caused this!"

Robin blinked at me. He quirked a smile, although

it seemed sad. Not that his being sad helped anything. In fact, it fueled the anger inside me.

"No, I didn't," he said. "I tried to stop you, if you remember."

I wracked my brain, trying to do exactly that. He'd appeared out of nowhere, saying that I shouldn't make wishes in a Faerie Ring. But then he'd kept talking to me, keeping me in that Ring… And me, stupid me…

Argh, I just wanted to punch him in his pretty face.

"You tricked me!" I decided.

He raised an eyebrow at that. "Really?" he asked. "You think I tricked you?"

"You kept talking to me. I mean, you could have just warned me and I would have left. Trust me, you freaked me out enough for me to run all the way back to my car."

"If I wanted you to make the wish, I could have just let you finish it the first time," he said. "Or did you forget that too?"

Was that the way it happened? It all felt fuzzy to me. The end result was the same, and he was the closest thing I had to laying the blame on someone else. Someone who wasn't me.

"I didn't forget that," I snarled. Then, the outburst made tears prick up in my eyes again. "It's just…it's all my fault. Alaina's baby is missing and—and…"

"Mortals and their placing blame," Robin sighed. He patted the spot next to him on the bench. "Come sit back down. I think you're going to melt or set the world on fire if you don't calm down."

I looked at him through my watery mess of tears and then I sat down.

"Oh *now* you listen to me," he sighed. He combed a hand through his unruly ginger hair.

"How do I fix this?" I asked.

"Fix what?"

"How do I get Alaina's baby back?"

Robin considered my question for a beat before shaking his head. "There's no way. The pixies took the baby, and there's no way."

"So the baby is alive?"

"We're not killers. Well, most of us." He considered that for moment. "Okay, maybe all of us are killers, but I'm fairly sure that the baby is alive. Pixies are tricky, but they don't kill the innocent."

"That's supposed to make me feel better?"

"Well, yeah."

"I need to get the baby back from them. Where are they?"

He scoffed. "You? Get the baby from them?" Then he went silent, making me look up at him. I thought he was trying to trick me again, but this time, he didn't look mischievous at all.

In fact, he looked slightly terrified.

"How do I rescue the baby?" I asked.

"No," Robin said firmly, shaking his head. "Absolutely not." He stood up and started walking away.

Anger propelled me to my feet and I followed him. I wasn't going to let him get away with just half-answers. Oh no, he was going to speak all right.

"How?" I demanded.

"Nunya."

"'Nunya'?" I repeated incredulously. "As in 'none of your business'? Did you really just say that?"

"Yep. Because it is nunya."

Ugh, infuriating.

"No, this is all my...nunya," I exclaimed. "Wait, I can just wish for the baby back, right?"

He glanced back at me. "Really, you didn't learn your lesson the first time? A wish requires a sacrifice and getting that baby back will require a bigger sacrifice than before. Plus, I'm not the one you should talk to about making wishes. I don't do that stuff, and I can't grant you that wish anyways, so don't even try."

"What about other faeries?"

"Seriously?"

I groaned in frustration.

He shook his head and turned away to go further into the glade ahead of me. No, he was *not* going to walk away like that.

I grabbed his arm and whirled him around to face me. "Listen," I demanded. I raised a fist and extended my finger at him. "I have magick now. And I don't know how to use it properly. So you'd better tell me what I can do, or else I'm going to see just how magickal I can be."

Amusedly, he smiled down at me. "You're really threatening me with your finger?" He flicked his eyes to my index finger.

I bristled. "I don't know what I can do with it."

"Nothing to me, Tinkerbell. I am one of the oldest faeries around, so trust me when I say I can take away your magick. And it wouldn't do any good even if I told you where they were."

With something between a grunt and a scream, I released him. "Please just tell me. I…I have to fix this. I have to save that baby."

He watched me for a few long, agonizing seconds. Finally, he sighed and scratched at his head. "You'd have to get the baby in Tir na nÓg."

"Tir na nÓg?"

I didn't even know what the heck that meant. Was it a place? Or a town? Or something else entirely?

"See, I told you it wouldn't do any good if you knew. You probably don't even know what it is." He leaned towards me. "It's a *realm* that mortals can't find by themselves. You wouldn't last two minutes by yourself."

I licked my lips. "Then take me there."

He blinked at my reaction. "What?" At least I surprised him.

My heart thudded in my chest. "Take me there. This is kind of your fault anyways." I wasn't so sure about that, but maybe I could guilt him into taking me there. I certainly had enough guilt to spread around.

"You're crazy."

"I'm desperate."

"Desperate, eh?" He stroked his chin as he looked slyly at me. "Does that mean you are asking me for a favor?"

A favor? Warning bells went off in my mind, something I'd read or heard a long time ago. That asking favors of faeries was never a good thing. Like he might come back and ask for my firstborn child. Or my house. Or any number of things that I cherished.

But none of that mattered at the moment. What mattered was getting Alaina's baby back.

"Yeah, I'm asking for a favor." My throat was dry as I said it.

Our gazes met again, and he watched me curiously. My insides squirmed under his keen, green-eyed scrutiny.

He clapped his hands once and rubbed them together. "Excellent."

He then grabbed my hand and the world around me went dark.

I didn't even have time to text Jordyn that I'd be back as soon as I could.

CHAPTER 5

"OH, YEAH, I FORGOT THAT MORTALS DON'T travel very well. Sorry, Tinkerbell."

For the second time in just a few hours. I emptied everything in my stomach. Which wasn't much, considering that Mom's pork casserole was somewhere by the side of the highway.

I sat back on my haunches and wiped the last of the spittle from my lips. I still felt sick and gross, like I'd been on a fishing boat too long, but that was the least of my worries as I looked around.

My blood ran cold and I couldn't process what my brain was seeing.

"Where are we?" I whispered.

Robin crossed his arms and nodded his head towards the scene that lay before me. "Tir na nÓg. Remember?"

Oh I remembered. I knew that I was Abigail Murphy, seventeen years old, and I lived in Centerburg, Florida. And I knew that we weren't on Earth anymore.

We were at the edge of a large cliff, and one quick glance told me that I didn't want to wander any further towards the edge. Nothingness and clouds lay below.

Impossibly green grass stretched out before us. The color was so brilliant, as if too much blue and teal got mixed up in the color palette when this scenery was painted in. Streams and rivers with blue, almost purple, glittering water spiderwebbed their way through the landscape, ending in waterfalls that cascaded off the side of the cliffs. Dense trees lay about a hundred yards before us, and beyond that, cliffs rose above the forest, dotted with buildings. Above everything was a bluish night sky. Only it wasn't nighttime. We were in an ethereal, even light.

I even saw a rainbow.

"Oh my god," I whispered, as I looked over the edge of the horizon.

Earth peeked over the edge, like it was the moon or the sun. It was huge, like some sort of overlord watching us here.

I got to my feet, my legs feeling weak underneath me. "We're not on Earth anymore?"

"We're in Tir na nÓg," Robin repeated. "The Land of the Young. Like you wanted."

Like that made sense. Because *none* of this was making any sense.

I looked around us, spinning around on my heel. I had to make an effort to stop myself, or else I'd keep spinning. This whole new world was dizzying.

"Are we on an island?" I asked stupidly. It felt like the ground wobbled slightly as I moved. "A floating island?"

"Yeah."

"You act like I should have already known all this."

"You were the one who wanted to come here. I even warned you. *Again*." He quirked a smile at me and cocked his head. "Still want to be here, Tinkerbell?"

I gulped, trying to calm the panic that threatened to explode. Apparently I hadn't thought this all the way through. I was in a strange land. With a strange, gorgeous faerie boy. Trying to get back Alaina's baby.

I was in over my head, way over my head, and I was powerless to take care of myself.

Stop it. You're not powerless.

I had magick now, even if I didn't know the full extent of it or how to safely use it. I knew that the pixies had gotten their sacrifice, and I knew that I had been powering my nightlight. Not that nightlight powers did a whole lot of good here, but maybe…*maybe*…

I held up my hand and willed the magick to my open palm. It was hard, and it felt like I drained myself, trying to focus on that one point in my entire body. At first, nothing happened.

Then finally, a spark erupted and a small, glowing flame appeared, hovering above my hand. I yelped in surprise and lost my concentration. The little fire immediately extinguished.

"Well, I'll be," Robin said, appreciatively, breaking into my thoughts. "Tinkerbell is not as helpless as she seems."

"I have fire magick," I said, stunned.

"Apparently," Robin said.

"Fire magick."

"Yeah?"

"You don't understand," I said, shaking my head. "My family has always used earth-based magick. My mom, my sister, my aunt, my grandma…"

"Uh-huh?"

"No one's ever had fire magick!" I gulped. "This isn't natural."

To my surprise, Robin put an arm around my shoulders. "Listen, Tinkerbell. You're dealing with faeries now. Nothing about this is natural. This is all faerie magick now."

I held my breath, so I didn't have to breathe in his sweet, earthy scent. It was tempting. I'd never been this close to such a good-looking guy in my entire life, and here he was helping me and –

Wait a second, this isn't insta-love is it?

Oh my god, I was turning into one of those mopey teenagers in books, the kind of girl that falls in love with the wrong guy the first time she sees him.

No, you're not, I told myself firmly. Just because he was handsome in a sinfully gorgeous way, that didn't mean I was head over heels in love with him. That would just be stupid on my part. He was here only because he expected something out of me later.

Just thinking about it made me shudder. I twisted away from him.

"Yeah, I know nothing about this is natural," I said, my voice slightly hoarse. Robin quirked an eyebrow at my change of demeanor, but waited for me to continue. "But that's why I have you here," I said, giving him a firm nod.

He gave me a devilish smile that totally did *not* make my heart flutter. "Yeah, sure," he said. "That's exactly why you have me here."

He pushed past me before I could say anything else. I was still in such deep thought that he turned around and looked back at me.

"Coming, Tinkerbell?"

That nickname was really starting to get old.

***

"WHERE ARE WE GOING?" I GRUMBLED.

I'd only been following Robin for a half hour and I'd learned one thing already: faerie boy never shuts up. He kept running his mouth, and while the terrain in Tir na nÓg wasn't especially treacherous, I had to watch my step in order not to step on anything that could have been a faerie.

You'd think it would have been easy to walk through a faerie wood. Everything here was magickal, from the air to the trees to the grass, too much for me to really digest. But I quickly realized that at any given point, a flower could really be a faerie or a rock was actually the shell of a turtle-faerie. I had the scratches on my calves from one such faerie that I had stepped on earlier.

Robin had thought that was hilarious.

It wasn't.

Now, Robin pointed at a spot ahead of us that I could just barely see peeking through the trees. There was a castle of sorts towards the center of the island, although I couldn't get a good look at it.

"We're going to the Spring Court first to see if they've seen or heard anything about an unborn human baby in Tir na nÓg. And if they haven't heard anything, then we go to the Summer Court, and hope that the baby is there."

"And if the baby isn't?" I asked breathlessly, fearing the answer. He had somehow gotten so far ahead of me in our walk. I didn't know how that happened. Time seemed to move at a weird clip here.

Robin stopped and waited for me to catch up at the top of a large rock. The light silhouetted him as he looked down at me, casting him in a soft hazy light that lit up his red hair like fire. I gulped back the lump in my throat as I started scrambling up the rock.

"You'd better hope the baby is in the Spring or Summer Courts," he told me. He extended a hand. I hesitated for just one moment before grabbing it, and then he hefted me up to the top of the rock, like I weighed nothing.

Our eyes met for the briefest moment before he turned away. I hoped he couldn't hear my heart pounding.

"Because if the baby isn't in the Spring or Summer

Courts," he continued, "then it's in the Autumn or Winter Courts. And we do *not* want to be dealing with their denizens."

"Why not?"

"Because they're the more…mischievous of the faeries. They dislike humans."

Well, that was a problem.

"So they're the bad guys?"

He shrugged. "Not necessarily the bad guys, but they're dark faeries who live in dark lands. You see, in the Spring and Summer Courts, it's always beautiful and bright. Autumn is perpetually stuck in early evening, while the Winter Court is stuck in at that point of night when it's the darkest." He shuddered.

"So the sun never shines there?" That sounded like a horrible place.

"No. You can imagine how that impacts a faerie's psyche. They follow different rules. It's not just good or evil. They just do their own thing. And lots of times, that's not good for mortals."

So I crossed my metaphorical fingers that Alaina's baby was in the Spring or Summer Courts.

"Which court do you belong to?" I asked.

"Pardon?" Now he looked back at me curiously.

"Are you a part of the Spring or Summer Courts?" I hoped he wasn't in the other ones. He wouldn't be helping me if he was in the Autumn or Winter ones, right?

Then again, he was only here so I would owe him a

favor.

A wicked smile came to his lips. "What do you think, Tinkerbell?"

"I…I have no idea."

He snickered and kept moving. "The pixies that took your friend's baby are solitary faeries," he continued without answering my question.

"Solitary faeries?" I asked, tripping over a root.

"Do you mind?" the face in the tree attached to the root growled at me.

"Sorry," I mumbled as I cowered away from it. I hurried to catch up with my guide, who didn't miss a beat.

"Solitary faeries live in the mortal world," he explained. "In your woods, in your households, in your backyards, pretty much everywhere humans are. But I think they took the baby to win favor with one of the Faerie Courts and rejoin the Faerie world."

"You mean Tir na nÓg?"

"Yes, Tir na nÓg. I think you just say it because you like those words." He pushed a branch out of the way for me, a courtesy he hadn't done up until now.

"Why would that win favor in the Faerie Courts?"

Robin let out a breath. "Because," he said finally, "some ruling monarchs like to adopt human babies. Take them under their wing. Raise them as a squire or to be treated like a doll. Or even for…*other* reasons. It's happened before."

I mentally gagged, because I didn't want to think of

the other reasons. "So the court that wants the baby will accept them into the Court?"

He nodded.

"What's wrong with being solitary fae? Why do they want to go back to Tir na nÓg?"

He pointed to the Earth hovering on the horizon. It hadn't moved since we started walking. "Because your world is being corrupted with human pollution, and it is making it harder for fae to live there."

Though I wasn't cold, I found myself shivering. I rubbed my arms to try to dispel my unease.

I forgot to recycle every bottle, every sheet of paper. I littered sometimes. I remembered Aunt Margaret lamenting that earth magick was a bit off lately due to climate change.

I just hadn't thought more into it. And now…

"I'm sorry," I whispered. Even though it was a far bigger problem than just me, I was at fault for it too. I furiously wiped at my eyes, trying to keep tears from leaking. I was crying a lot tonight, apparently.

So many reasons to feel guilty.

Robin didn't say anything as he watched me, his green eyes glittering. "Mortals have fascinated me for a long time," he said softly.

"What do you mean by that?"

"You are very…conflicting creatures," he admitted. "You don't take care of your environment, yet you leap at the slim possibility of saving a baby that isn't even your own. It's like you mean well, but you are so misguided."

I nodded. "That's putting it lightly."

"But if there's one thing I've learned about mortals, it's that you can *be* guided."

"Like guiding me through Faerieland?"

"Yeah." He looked amused. "Like guiding you through Faerieland."

CHAPTER 6

I SENSED THE CHANGE IN THE AIR AS SOON AS we stepped out into a meadow. The grassy field led up to a tranquil castle nestled among some rocks at the mouth of a babbling creek. The air here was lazy. Breathing it in made me want to lay down in the grass and sigh happily, curl up and fall asleep. The sun in this part of the faerie world was stronger than the rest of the island, like it was perpetually helping daffodils and daisies shake off winter.

Although winter hadn't been here in a long time.

"Spring always was the nicest Court," Robin muttered. He stuffed his hands in his pockets as he nodded at the castle. "Everything's always perfect." He looked none too happy about that.

"Spring is my favorite season," I said offhandedly.

"Of course it is."

"Well, it's when winter is finally done. Everything's blooming and pretty. The weather is perfect…"

"…and the ruler here is crazy," Robin finished for me. In fact, he looked miserable.

"Who is it?" I asked.

He scoffed, as if the name tasted bad on his tongue.

"Queen Titania."

"That sounds familiar," I said, although I couldn't pick up where I'd gotten it from.

Robin patted my shoulder. "When all this is done, do yourself a favor, Tinkerbell, and read *A Midsummer Night's Dream*. Old Will got a lot of things wrong, but you'd at least have an inkling of what's about to happen."

Who knew that high school reading could have been helpful in a situation like this?

"Okay," I said quietly.

"Oh, and I forgot to say…" He looked down at me. "Don't eat or drink anything here."

As if right on cue, my stomach rumbled unhappily. We'd been in Tir na nÓg for hours, it seemed, and I'd thrown up what I had for dinner. My stomach was empty and the very thought of food made my mouth water.

"Here? As in Tir na nÓg? Why?"

Robin groaned. "Because if a mortal like you ever wanted to leave Tir na nÓg, you can't have any sort of sustenance here. It creates a bond and it won't let you leave."

I gulped nervously through a dry throat. "Okay."

Robin looked back towards the castle. "Let's get this over with. I'm sure her Highness is going to be *so* happy to see me."

So they had a history. Well this was going to be fun.

"Why'd we come here first then?" I asked.

"Because it was the most likely place," Robin

answered. "Titania loves her changelings."

"What's a changeling?"

"A child stolen by faeries. Sound familiar?" His eyes glittered as he said that.

"Oh."

He grinned and started walking through the meadow, tiny faeries leaping out of the way of our feet. They floated like little tiny multicolored fireflies, and I watched them, transfixed. I blinked and the spell was broken, and I hurried to match Robin's pace.

He seemed amused.

"You have no idea what you've gotten into, you realize that, right?"

"I'm realizing that now," I replied honestly. "How is it so different than the human world?" I was familiar with the foundations of magick in my world, but this was an entirely new ballgame for me.

"Because this is where anything is possible. Always remember that, Tinkerbell. You could get into big trouble if you don't pay attention."

We walked for a few minutes as I mulled over his words. The castle seemed to grow in size the closer we got to it, and I felt panicked at the possibility of the baby being there. Or, even worse, if the baby wasn't there. I had to fill the silence, otherwise I would go crazy.

I tried to make conversation. "Can I ask you something?"

"You're asking a lot of questions already, Tinkerbell,

so shoot." He sounded amused.

"Why do you always call me 'Tinkerbell'?"

He looked at me, his green eyes raking over my face and I could feel my cheeks deepen in a blush. "You remind me of her," he said finally.

"Is she real?"

"No." He laughed mockingly. "She's a fairy tale."

I frowned, feeling let down by that. "Well, you're like a Peter Pan, who's a villain," I retorted.

"What makes me a villain?"

"You frighten me."

The words popped out before I could stop them, but it stopped Robin in his tracks. His face was unreadable as he gazed at me, and I swallowed, feeling self-conscious again.

"Listen, Tinkerbell—*Abby*," he corrected himself and licked his lips. "I—"

"Why, if it isn't Robin Goodfellow!" an impossibly high-pitched voice screeched, interrupting whatever he was going to say. Disappointment fluttered in my stomach.

"Hello, Mustardseed," Robin said, his voice now bored.

"You have a lot of nerve showing your face here after everything you did!" I still couldn't see who or what Mustardseed was, as the voice seemed to be coming from every direction.

"I was working for my king," Robin answered. "You'd do the same for Titania."

"Yes, but she is better than Oberon," Mustardseed's voice quipped, sounding highly offended.

Robin snorted, letting the voice know exactly what he thought of Titania. "I'm sure any loyal subject thinks that way about their ruler." He nodded to me. "Now, if you're done trying to posture, would you mind showing your ugly face so that the little lady could see you?"

"What little lady—*Oh!*"

From out of nowhere, a young child's face popped into existence two inches from my nose, like it was inspecting me. I shrieked and stumbled backwards. The faerie in front of me was persistent, inspecting me, and watching me like I was a unicorn. Then I wondered if there were any unicorns in Tir na nÓg and I thought that if there were, they probably wouldn't be as magickal to faeries as they are to humans.

"You brought a mortal here?" Mustardseed fretted. "Oh, Titania isn't going to like this."

"Why wouldn't Titania like me here?" I asked. I tried stepping out of the faerie's way, but it kept coming in closer to inspect me.

"And the mortal talks too!" Mustardseed bemoaned. "Oh no."

I couldn't tell if Mustardseed was a boy or a girl. It was only the length of my hand and green-skinned with a loin cloth made up of lilies and a shirt made up of leaves. Gossamer wings allowed it to fly around my head like some sort of satellite in orbit.

It got old really quick.

"Relax," Robin said. As if noticing that I was unhappy being inspected like this, he plucked the faerie out of the air and held it aloft. "The mortal is just here to ask Titania a question, and we'll be on our merry way soon after that."

"There is no 'merry way' with you, Robin," Mustardseed lamented. "You always find ways of mucking things up."

Robin shrugged and released the little guy. "It's in my nature. Now, are you going to take us to your wise and kind ruler or are we going to have to get the bug spray out to shut you up?"

"Why, I never!" Mustardseed protested.

Robin rolled his eyes. "C'mon Tinkerbell. And once we get to the Spring Court, let me do the talking."

I was actually very impressed with how he had handled things, so I suppressed a giggle as I sidestepped the little faerie and caught up with Robin, who didn't even look back once as we walked to the castle. Mustardseed let his unhappiness be known the entire time, but it was far more fun to ignore the faerie and ruffle some feathers, than anything else.

The castle was more of an open-air building. Columns entwined with ivy delineated the castle grounds, and trees wove together to make some semblance of a structure. For the most part, it was like flowers and ferns made up the castle.

In a word, it was breathtaking, unlike anything I had

ever seen before. I went to a botanical garden once. The flowers had been in full bloom, gorgeous, and immaculately displayed. It was enough to make a huge impression on my then-five-year-old mind.

But it was nothing like this.

I remembered that Jordyn had made that trip a little more special by using a little bit of her earth magick to create a doll entirely made out of flowers. I cherished that doll and even dried it to preserve it as much as possible. I still kept it underneath my bed, although it wasn't as pretty as that one day.

I missed Jordyn. I wondered if she was worried about me or if she had noticed I was missing. Would she think that I had been kidnapped? Or that something had happened to me?

Was human time the same as Faerie time?

I chewed on my bottom lip. Robin noticed my somber mood, but didn't say anything. For once, I was glad that he didn't quip or make fun of me.

A guard stood at the door, glaring down at us. I could only describe him as a troll, as he was about twelve feet tall with warty skin and a bad odor that made my eyes water.

There were apparently a lot of different kinds of faeries.

"Robin Goodfellow," the troll rumbled in a voice that was almost too low for me to hear. He suspiciously eyed my companion. "What brings you here?"

Robin crossed his arms and cocked his head. "We're

here to see Titania."

"It's *Queen* Titania to you!" Mustardseed cried in his high-pitched voice, panicked that Robin hadn't addressed the queen correctly. "I'm so sorry, Gigamarth. I tried stopping them and—"

"Tried and failed, Mustardseed," said a lovely voice that wasn't the troll's.

Just when I thought things couldn't get any weirder, a sparkle of faerie dust appeared in the space between us and the troll. A heart-breakingly beautiful woman stepped out from the dust and crossed her arms as she shrewdly looked at Robin.

"I suspected as much," she said. Her voice lilted with each word, like a harp had married with vocal chords, pretty while sounding unimpressed with Robin in front of her. "Robin Goodfellow, I haven't seen your carcass in these parts for a long time."

That beautiful voice sounded angry. I was so transfixed, my mind panicked about disappointing her, rather than worrying about what effect that would have on me in the end.

"Just doing my own thing, your grace," Robin said, unaffected by her.

Her gaze landed on me, and her upper lip twitched in a sneer. "Well, well, well," she said. "What do we have here?"

CHAPTER 7

THE LUSTER OF TITANIA'S BEAUTY WORE OFF after about five minutes.

Sure, she was taller than me with a waterfall of blond hair that would make a Pantene Pro-V model jealous. Her eyes were icy blue and her skin flawless. She wore a dress made out of blue flowers that looked like it had been woven by a thousand tiny faerie hands.

She was beautiful. But I quickly found out that she was a bitch.

And that she did *not* like me one bit.

I still had to shake my head and remind myself every once in a while that she was a faerie queen who did not want me here. Her manner was at odds with her beauty, giving me a headache the entire time we talked to her.

We were in a courtyard inside the castle which acted as her throne room. The sun here warmed our skin and it felt peaceful the entire time. There were many different kinds of spring faeries here, from ones that were smaller than Mustardseed to those that were bigger than the troll out front. They all looked at me like I was some sort of alien. I guess, in a way, I was, but that was no excuse for how Titania was treating me.

She massaged her temples as she looked down at us from her ornate, natural throne.

Another thing I picked up on very quickly: she *hated* Robin.

"Why would I be interested in an unborn baby?" she asked in a bored voice. "I'd have to magickally incubate it until it's done, and you know I have no time for that."

"You've wanted stranger things," Robin countered. "You remember that changeling you wanted, but Oberon wanted for his knight?"

"That boy was mine," Titania snarled, her face twisting into a mask that looked nothing like her beautiful self. The transformation happened so quickly, I blinked, taken aback. Titania took a few moments to compose herself, her long nails drumming on the arm rest of her throne. "And if Oberon had just agreed, none of this would have happened."

"What happened with the changeling?" I asked. Robin shot me a glare, but I didn't care. As I figured, I was already pretty deep here in the Spring Court.

Titania watched me as her fingers incessantly drummed on the armrest. "Oberon," she said, "my *ex*-husband, sought to steal a mortal child that was rightfully mine. I never forgave him for that. Which is why there is now a Spring and Summer Court."

"Hail, the Spring Court and its benevolent ruler, Queen Titania," the faeries around me chanted in unison. I jumped at the unexpected cacophony.

Robin rolled his eyes. "So you have no idea where this new human baby is?" he asked for the seventeenth time since we arrived. He asked it in a different way every time, as if he was trying to catch Titania in a lie.

This time, she picked up on his tactic and she shot daggers at him with her eyes. "Of course I have no idea where this unborn baby is!" she sneered.

"You keep talking to her like you expect she's lying," I whispered to Robin, "but I thought that faeries can't lie." Somewhere in a fairy tale, I'd read that.

He raised an amused eyebrow. "You've got another thing coming to you if you think faeries can't lie," he whispered back. "They do." He turned back to the faerie queen. "A lot."

"What reason would I have to lie?" Titania thundered, angry that he would suggest such a thing. "Besides, I have no room in my court for another bunch of pixies. You know how they swarm you when they panic, and ruin your clothing and scratch your skin."

A few of the smaller faeries in the courtyard stopped flitting around so much, and I thought they were frowning at Titania. Apparently she had just insulted them with that comment.

She'd fit right in with American politicians.

Robin glanced at me. "Sorry Tinkerbell," he said, shrugging. "I guess we'll have to head over to the Summer Court."

Titania sat a little straighter at his comment, narrowing her eyes. "You're going to go see Oberon?"

"Next stop on our rescue mission."

Deliberately, she rose from her throne and stalked towards us. Robin didn't seem bothered by her advance, but I found myself cowering away from her. Her anger was palpable as she closed in on us.

"Tell him to stop sending me gifts and trying to win me back," Titania told Robin.

"Why don't you tell him yourself?" Robin asked. "I'm not your messenger boy."

"But you're *his*," Titania said.

"Look, your ladyship, no one tells me what to do."

"Then why are you leading a mortal into our lands?" Titania gestured to me, as if I couldn't hear them speaking.

Robin gave me a sidelong glance. "I'm doing it in exchange for a favor," he said simply.

While I knew it was the truth, the way he put it hurt deep in my chest. I knew that he was a faerie, and a trickster faerie at that, but I'd hoped that he was doing it for more reasons than just my owing him something at the end of all of this.

But that was how things were here. It was the law of the land.

Titania considered this for a moment before allowing a small smile to creep onto her features. It was not a kind smile and it chilled me to the bone.

"I see," she said. She turned her attention to me, fully

taking my appearance in. "I can sense that you have a bit of magick in you, human girl."

"It's Abby," I corrected, although my voice didn't sound as strong as I would have liked. Still, it had the effect of making Titania pause and behind her, Robin gave me an approving look.

"Fire magick, isn't it?" Titania asked.

I nodded.

Titania touched a finger to her chin, deep in thought. "I could always use a little bit of fire in my court in case I need to light a fire under Oberon's ass." She extended a hand to me, and for a moment, I had no idea what she meant by it, but she gave me the warmest smile ever and beckoned with her fingers. "Join my court, human child, and stay in a land of eternal spring where you will never grow old and your powers will be appreciated for all eternity."

The warm, inviting way she said it caught me off guard, and my hand was already reaching out to take hers in a handshake before I stopped myself.

What the hell was I thinking?

I blinked the confusion away from my brain and shook my head. "I'm...good..." It was incredibly hard to say that, like I was saying it through a hoarse throat.

I heard a sigh of relief, that I first thought was me, but then I saw that Robin looked immensely satisfied. The sigh had come from him.

Meanwhile, Titania frowned at me, obviously not

happy with my answer. "Girl," she said. "You don't know what you're turning down."

"Probably," I agreed, "but once I find Alaina's baby, I want to return to the human world."

"You won't ever die," she hissed. "You'll be treated as a hero. A wonderful servant that the people of my court can rely on."

Yeah, exactly why I don't want to take you up on that.

"I understand, but I have my own duties to perform. Mainly finishing up high school, which is probably harder than defending your court, your Highness."

Robin snorted in amusement. Titania schooled her face into a sugary-sweet expression that made my teeth ache.

"Well, if you insist on leaving my court," she said, "you should probably pack some provisions for your journey. I know Tir na nÓg may seem small to a new traveler, but it's far bigger than you could ever imagine. You'll need sustenance in order to make it."

Again, as if on cue, my traitorous stomach growled again. I felt the entire court chuckle amusedly, even though Robin's face spelled doom.

"We don't need anything, your Grace," he said quickly, trying to step in between Titania and me.

"Nonsense, Robin," she chided, shooing him away. "This is a human girl who needs to eat. Isn't that right, child?"

I opened my mouth to say that I was fine and that I

wasn't a child, but Titania held up her hand and conjured up a red, juicy apple that made my mouth water. I never understood how, in the fairy tales, Snow White would take a random apple from a stranger and eat it, but now I did. This magickal fruit was like a black hole that sucked me in.

My mouth instantly watered, and I lost myself.

As if knowing the effect it had on me, Titania pushed the apple towards me. Towards my mouth, where I could just taste the fruit and the juice filling my mouth. Just one bite, and I'd be fine.

One bite…

What are you doing? my subconscious screamed at me. *What did Robin tell you? Don't eat it. Stop it!*

Stop it!

I heaved a quick breath and stepped away, tearing my gaze from the apple. I pushed a bit of magick towards it to remove the fruit from my sight, and it exploded in Titania's hand with a burst of fire. The faerie queen shrieked in surprise as juice and apple bits got all over her.

At least now, it looked far less appetizing.

"I'm good," I said throatily. I was going to be all right, even if my stomach told me I wasn't. "I think Robin and I should go. Thank you for the offer, but we have places to be."

I grabbed his arm and we rushed out of the throne room. The court went into a frenzy as we left, some faeries chattering about what just happened, and others moving to help their queen. Titania herself shrieked in anger, but

I shut it out as we kept moving. Luckily no one moved to stop us, or else we would have had no hope of getting out of there.

Once out of the glade and into the main part of the castle, Robin took over and ushered me out, turning at all the right places and not getting lost, which I surely would have done as my mind wasn't working correctly.

When we spilled out into the meadow in front of the castle, he let go of my arm and I collapsed on the ground, glad to be out of there.

"I guess that's one way your magick has helped us," Robin said amusedly. "That's the second time you've listened to me, which saved your life."

"She was trying to put a spell on me," I croaked, holding my empty midsection. Every sensation was coming back to me. I was tired, hungry, and shivering even though the temperature here was a nice seventy degrees. "I thought she didn't like humans."

"She doesn't."

"So why was she trying to keep me there?"

Robin fell silent, watching me for a few heartbeats before sighing and shaking his head. "She's trying to get back at me."

"What does that have to do with you?"

He stuffed his hands into his pockets and looked away, his cheeks reddening as if he was embarrassed. "Beats me."

Except I could guess that it didn't beat him. That he

knew why. Or at least, that's what I thought. Everything seemed so fuzzy right now.

"I don't know if I can do this another three times," I murmured.

"If you want to find that baby, you might have to," Robin said pointedly.

He held a hand out to me, and I took it. He pulled me to my feet and I stumbled as I my legs were shaky. He held onto me longer than was necessary, making sure that I'd be able to handle myself. But being this close to him was just as intoxicating as that apple was, and I was sure he could hear my heart pounding in my chest.

No, dammit. You are not experiencing insta-love, Abby, I firmly told myself. I just wished I would listen.

"Thanks," I whispered, stepping away. "I don't think I like Spring anymore."

Robin offered me a small smile, but otherwise his face was unreadable.

"So, Tinkerbell, are you ready to take on the Summer Court?"

I had to be, didn't I?

CHAPTER 8

THERE WAS AT LEAST ONE THING THAT Titania had been right about. For being a floating island, Tir na nÓg was immense. We were lucky that our entry point to the faerie world had been close to the Spring Court. From there, the trek to the Summer Court seemed to take forever, which was made worse by the fact that my stomach seemed to be eating itself. Seeing that apple in Titania's hand had set my body off on a rebellious streak to make me want to eat anything within my grasp.

And the faerie world had plenty of things that looked edible. Like *Willy Wonka and the Chocolate Factory,* I could see things hanging in the trees that resembled fruit, or berries on bushes. Aside from the shock of how different this world was than ours, I was overwhelmed by things beckoning me to eat them.

Luckily Robin knew the way and kept talking to me to take my mind off the emptiness in my stomach. At least it was working a little bit.

"How much further?" I asked for what seemed like the thousandth time. "I would have thought that the Spring and Summer Courts would have been closer to each other."

"You need to learn patience, Tinkerbell," he said. "We're basically walking across the entire faerie world on this little quest of yours, and you saw how much Titania hates Oberon. You think she would have put her kingdom close to his?"

He had a point there, but that didn't help make this seem any better.

"Is this kind of like going home for you then?" I asked. "Going to the Summer Court?"

Robin blinked at me curiously. "What makes you say that?"

Now I was confused. "Well, they were all acting like Oberon was your master or something like that."

He threw back his head and laughed. "Trust me, Tinkerbell, no one is Robin Goodfellow's master. Not a faerie king or queen. Not even a wee mortal girl that he made a bargain with. So you'd better remember that."

I chewed the inside of my cheek as we walked. Rather than risk having my empty stomach make another embarrassing noise, I decided to fill the silence. "So, what court are you a part of, then?"

"My own," Robin said darkly.

"Your own?"

"Yeah." He shrugged. "I don't like being told what to do."

After meeting Titania and seeing how she did things, I was hoping that the Summer Court would be more welcoming. Not only that, but if Alaina's baby wasn't in the Summer Court, then we'd have to go to the Autumn and Winter Courts, where Robin had said things were even worse. I didn't know if I'd be able to survive that, especially with the long walks between places.

If I did survive all of these different courts and I still couldn't find the baby, I…

Well, I had no idea what I'd do.

As if Robin could read my thoughts on my face, he said, "Hey, we'll figure this out."

I blinked, feeling tears stream down my face. I hadn't even noticed them there until I blinked. I wiped at them furiously.

I wished Jordyn was here. She'd know what to do, and she'd know how to deal with faerie queens like Titania. She knew how to deal with heavy stuff like this, because she'd done it before. I shook my head. No, Jordyn had messed up badly before and fixed it. This was my mess to fix. It had to be me.

Even though I could fail.

"Mortals cry far more than faeries do," Robin observed curiously. To my utter surprise, he reached out and brushed another tear off my cheek. His touch sent shivers down my spine, and I watched, amazed, as the droplet hung on Robin's finger as he inspected it like it was some new species of beetle.

"What good does crying do?" he asked quietly.

"Nothing," I whispered. "But sometimes I can't stop

it."

"Hey, Tinkerbell," he started. His eyes flicked to me and then his expression immediately changed. "Aw hell," he muttered, wiping the hand that held my tear on his pants.

"What—?" I started to ask, but a loud rumbling from above cut me off.

"WHY, IF IT ISN'T ROBIN GOODFELLOW."

I looked up and screamed.

So far, I'd met pixies, faeries like Mustardseed and others that I've nearly stepped on, Queen Titania and even Robin surprised me by popping out of nowhere. But none of them, not even the troll at the gates to the castle of the Spring Court had been as tall as a building.

This faerie was, if he actually was a faerie. I didn't know if there was a difference between faeries and giants, but this being fell squarely into the "giant" category regardless.

He was terrifying.

His head and face towered above the treetops overhead, so I luckily couldn't see his face, but that did nothing for the lower half. He was gnarled with leathery skin that resembled an elephant's, and he was the same gray color too. His feet, which smelled like rotting flesh, were wrapped in different animal hides with a thick cord holding them in place. Chains cuffed his ankles and wrapped around his legs. He held a club that was the size of my car at the end. One hit with that and I was a goner.

But that wasn't the worst part. He wore *heads* around

his waist, like they were some sort of chain mail that he had hoped to cover up his nether regions with. The heads ranged from humanoid to purely animals, and were all sorts of different sizes, from the size of my thumb to the size of the troll's head from earlier. And they were all just hanging together, dead.

"Hey! Tinkerbell!" Robin hissed. "Hush, or you're going to get yourself killed."

I clamped my hand to my mouth and staggered backward. Robin stepped in front of me to address the giant. Should I hide? Maybe it hadn't seen me. Maybe—

"Hey, Jack!" he shouted up at the giant. "What brings you outside of the Winter Court?"

"IT GOT BORING THERE," the giant rumbled back. "EVERYONE KNOWS ME IN THE WINTER COURT."

So this was one of the faeries that really hated humans. Great. If this was a sample of them, then I was doomed.

The ground shook when he spoke, like he was an earthquake all by himself. How the heck did he appear out of nowhere like that? Surely I would have seen him before then. Right?

Still, relief spread across my brain as I realized that he hadn't addressed my scream. Those hopes were quickly dashed when—

"WHAT WAS THAT SCREAM?" the giant rumbled.

Damn. He had heard me. I slowly backed away. I

had no idea what the giant's face looked like, but I hoped he was just paying attention to Robin. That was probably cowardly of me, but my faerie guide seemed like he could take care of himself.

"Just me screaming," Robin quipped. Behind his back, he was waving at me, directing me to a bunch of blue thorny bushes to our right. At least he was telling me to hide. "You surprised me, Jack."

Very cautiously, I started sidestepping my way over there. Adrenaline brought everything into hyper-realistic focus, and I could hear my heart pounding from fear.

"THAT SCREAM DIDN'T SOUND LIKE YOU."

"I'm good at changing my voice," Robin said. "I've been practicing. You know, scaring mortals."

"I HAVEN'T SCARED A MORTAL IN CENTURIES," the giant lamented, sounding genuinely sad. "I'VE JUST BEEN STUCK IN TIR NA NÓG SINCE MAB PUT A BAN ON VISITING THE HUMAN WORLD."

"Aw, I'm sorry to hear that big guy," Robin said, with false care. "I'm sure you'll figure it out."

I was nearly to the bush.

"HAVE YOU MET A MORTAL LATELY? MAYBE YOU CAN BRING ME BACK ONE TO EAT."

"Nope, not recently," Robin lied. "I've just been here, just like you."

"THAT'S NOT WHAT I HEARD. I HEARD—"

A loud crack sounded throughout the space,

impossibly loud. I could see Robin's posture stiffen as he winced at the sound. My foot had stepped on a branch. I hoped the giant hadn't heard it. Robin and I both froze.

Above us, the treetops parted and one giant eye peered through the canopy, blinking down at us, first at Robin, then at me.

"A MORTAL GIRL!" the giant yelled happily. "I'VE FOUND A MORTAL GIRL!"

"Run, Abby!" Robin yelled.

I was about to ask him where I could run when the giant club swung my way, cracking trees and bushes in its way. I yelped and dodged as the top of it smashed into the ground where I was just nanoseconds beforehand.

The giant roared. Obviously, he could tell that he hadn't hit me. He smashed the ground again, trying to get at me, this time close enough to send me sprawling.

"Dammit, Tinkerbell!" Robin yelled, pushing me out of the way. The club missed me and only grazed him, but that was enough to send him flying into the trees, out of sight and far away from me.

Oh my god, I was alone in the woods with a giant. I was hyperventilating, darkness edging into my vision as I contemplated what to do next. There was no hiding when a giant was after you.

So could I stop him in another way?

Magick. Use your fire magick.

I didn't have to use a phrase or draw a circle—my magick apparently worked differently than my family's. I held the spell in my head and threw it at the enormous wooden club, hoping against hope that it actually worked. The giant must have had that club for a long time, because the dead wood immediately took to the flame and ignited.

The giant howled in pain, dropping the fiery club, setting some nearby trees on fire. I didn't have time to worry about whether or not Robin had landed far enough away to be spared from the inferno.

I didn't see the huge hairy foot as it came my way. It connected right in my gut, knocking the air out of me as the giant literally kicked me across the forest.

Blackness edged in my vision, and I passed out before I landed.

I hate Tir na nÓg.

CHAPTER 9

IT WAS NIGHTTIME WHEN I FINALLY CAME TO my senses.

I groaned and rolled my head. My body felt stiff as a board from being kicked around the faerie realm. I lay in a heap at the bottom of a hill, dry autumn leaves surrounding me, making a nest for me to lay on. At least I landed somewhere soft, right?

Ugh, maybe it wasn't as soft as I originally thought.

I gingerly sat up, cringing as my abdomen ached in protest. I thought the giant's foot had cracked a few ribs. I could only manage a shallow breath because pain wracked through my body in warning.

Was anything else broken?

I took stock of myself, wincing with each and every new movement. There was only a little bit of blood from scratches, and I checked my stomach for bruises. No bones poking through my flesh and I could feel all ten fingers and toes. I think I had escaped without breaking anything important. I'm sure I didn't look too pretty though.

"Robin?" I asked through dry, chapped lips. My voice didn't sound like it was my own. "Robin?"

No answer.

I looked around, hoping that maybe he was playing a trick on me, that he was somewhere nearby laughing at my pain and the horrible state I was in. Please let that be the case, that he was a horrible person playing a trick on me, and not that he wasn't here.

"Robin?" I asked again, feeling my heart going into overdrive at the lack of response.

My voice echoed around me, and I could hear the humorous chitter chatter of faeries around me, but no Robin came to say that he was just around the corner.

Don't panic, don't panic.

I was alone in Tir na nÓg. Not only that, but based on how the trees looked like they were on fire with red and orange leaves that the wind plucked off their branches, I was somewhere in the Autumn Court. How, I didn't know. All I knew was that I was where the faeries hated humans. Where I was completely lost.

More tears came and I hunched forward despite the pain in my chest and cried.

***

IT TOOK A LITTLE WHILE FOR ME TO GET A handle on my sheer terror. The one good thing about being a Murphy was that I could only let so much despair swallow me before I had to do something about it. I had to figure out my next move before other faeries found me, and I didn't want a giant like the last one to find me alone.

I looked around and tried to determine where I was. From what I could tell, I was at the bottom of a hill, surrounded by huge trees that made me feel like I was tiny. Judging by the slope and the number of leaves, I had zero hope of being able to scale the hill and see where I was.

It was also dark outside, locked into an eternal twilight. I remembered Robin saying something about the different courts being perpetually stuck at different parts of the day. It looked like it was seven o'clock on an autumn day; there was no sunlight, but the sky hadn't reached its darkest point.

I was relieved that there was one thing I could do to help look around. I held up a hand and concentrated my new magick to my palm. A tiny spark erupted there, and I held a small flame in my hand. The wonder of being able to do that still amazed me, but I had to figure out how to get out of here.

The little flame lit up the immediate area around me, filling out the shadows that had been just out of reach before. I could see eyes of all shapes and sizes looking down at me, some curious and some malicious. Not the best feeling in the world, having a bunch of faeries watch you while you cried.

"Can anyone help me?" I asked.

A few of the eyes blinked at me, but no one responded. Better than having one attack me, but I needed some help.

"Can any of you help me find the Summer Court or a faerie named Robin Goodfellow? Please?" *I'm desperate.*

At first, nothing happened. I saw some of the eyes wink out of existence, while the others just kept watching me. I was about to cry out in frustration when…

A small bluish light appeared about twenty yards ahead of me, adding its light to my small, palm-held fire. It hovered in the air, just by itself, as if waiting for me patiently.

I didn't know much about faerie folklore, but my brain suddenly remembered a part in a movie that featured little lights floating like this.

"A will-'o-the-wisp," I murmured, amazed. If I remembered correctly, a will-'o-the-wisp guided travelers. In the movie, it guided the main character to something that didn't quite pan out as planned, but it did help out in the end.

Here's to hoping that it worked the same here.

"You want me to follow you?" I asked.

The will-'o-the-wisp hovered in an up-and-down motion, as if it nodded at me.

"Okay."

I slowly got to my feet, wincing with every step as my cracked ribs protested every movement. I was seriously hurt in a few different ways, but at least I could walk. If I could have a drink or something, that would be even better.

Still, Robin's warning about not having anything to eat or drink echoed in my mind. So I just dealt with it.

I made it to the will-'o-the-wisp, a bit disappointed that it hadn't moved ahead of me, like some sort of guide. Yet as soon I neared it, another will-'o-the-wisp winked into existence another twenty yards ahead of me.

"You want me to follow that one too?" I asked, even though I wasn't sure if the will-'o-the-wisp understood me. Of course, I didn't get a direct answer, but I took that as a sign to keep going.

Just like connect the dots, I told myself. *A big giant coloring book page of connect the dots. Except you're connecting it across the Autumn Court.* The absurdity of it made me laugh out loud. I'm sure the will-'o-the-wisp didn't appreciate that.

When I made it to the second will-'o-the-wisp, another came into existence beyond that, and it kept happening every time I got close to the next one. Where they were directing me, I had no idea, but it felt good just to be moving again. The will-'o-the-wisp never seemed to hurry me, and I stopped questioning what they were doing. They were little nightlights guiding my way through this mess.

At one point, the canopy of the woods broke, revealing the night sky. I stopped and allowed myself to gape up at the smattering of the stars. I lived an hour outside of Jacksonville in a decent-sized town, so while I could see the stars, they were never like this.

"I don't recognize any of the constellations," I murmured to myself. After a decade of looking up at my bedroom's ceiling, I should have been able to easily place where Ursa Major and Orion and other constellations were pinpointed into the sky. Instead, I saw groupings of stars that made no sense.

I shivered, suddenly feeling very cold and even more alone, if that was possible. At every opportunity, it felt like Tir na nÓg was trying to remind me that I wasn't in my world anymore. Something as vast and as simple as having a different sky at night frightened me on some sort of primal level.

I was all alone.

I forced myself to tear my eyes away from that night sky and pushed myself as hard as my cracked ribs would allow. The sooner I found and rescued Alaina's baby, the sooner I could go home and get away from this. The thought bothered me that I might never be able to see Robin again, but I pushed that from my mind.

It wasn't like we were going to date or anything, or even as if he *had* feelings for me. Because I certainly didn't—or, rather, it's not like these feelings were real. That was it. I was just overwhelmed and clung to the one person who helped me.

Once this was all said and done, life would go back to normal. Although he did want a favor out of me. Hopefully it would be as simple as giving him a cup of sugar or something. I doubted that seriously but what's a life without hope?

My head started aching at all of the different thoughts swirling through my brain, and I sucked down the pain.

The will-'o-the-wisp led me through the meadow, under the open sky for some time. I had no idea how long I was following them, but they always seemed patient beacons for me to follow.

I heard the babbling before I actually saw the stream that cut through the meadow. Was the will-'o-the-wisp ahead of me going to lead me along the stream to the Summer Court? Because civilizations were situated around water, right?

Yet as I got to the will-'o-the-wisp, I didn't see any more wink into existence. I stopped and looked around to see if any more of the blue lights had popped up. I frowned and did a full 360° trying to see if I could spot the next beacon of light.

Nothing.

Maybe it was across the stream? Although it looked too far for me cross, I stepped down to the bank and looked around anyway.

There was a woman standing knee-deep in the stream about sixty feet from where I was, silhouetted by the night.

I wasn't expecting anyone to be there at all, so I jumped when I spotted her, but managed not to shriek in fear this time. Maybe I was getting used to Tir na nÓg then.

Was this who the will-'o-the-wisps were leading me to? What if she was a bad faerie?

I looked back to the last wisp, which hadn't been joined by another one. So they did want me here. I clenched and unclenched my fingers, debating what I should do. I had fire magick. If she was a bad faerie, I was going to have to risk it and defend myself if that was the case.

But the will-'o-the-wisps wouldn't lead me here maliciously, would they?

"Hello?" I called.

The woman, who was bent over something in the stream, stopped and looked up at me. So far so good. I took a few steps towards her down the bank.

"Hi there!" I called. "I am trying to get to the Summer Court, but I got separated from my guide. Can you help me?"

I took a few more steps towards her, but then froze.

The woman—if she could be called that—had long stringy gray hair with no nose on her sallow face. She wore an old-timey cloak that was soaked in a substance that was darker than the water of the stream. Her hands held a garment stained with the same liquid as her cloak, and I realized that I had interrupted her scrubbing it in the stream.

Blood. She was washing blood out of someone's clothes.

My heart pounded in my ears as our gazes connected, only she didn't have eyes. She had deep black sockets that threatened to engulf me in their sad expression.

I tried backing up. I tried getting away, but my feet were rooted to the spot.

Then she opened her mouth and screamed.

The sound broke me out of my trance, and I grimaced, holding my hands to my ears. She just kept screaming, her voice never ending as it filled the night with the horrible sound.

She started walking towards me, treading through the water and leaving behind a trail of dark red in her wake, although her scream never stopped.

Something grabbed me by the upper arm and pulled me away from her. In one last try, she reached out for me before I was pulled out of sight and away from her. The scream went on for a little longer, and I shut my eyes against the horror of it. I never wanted to hear that again.

"Trust you to find the Bean-Nighe," a familiar voice said, trying to sound amused, but only sounding exhausted.

I looked up too see Robin's gaze boring into mine. He actually looked just as worse for wear as I did, his green eyes tired as he offered me a small smile. "You are pretty hard to track down when you want to be," he said softly.

Where had he come from? What had happened to him? Who was that woman?

All sorts of thoughts, but only one made its way to my lips as my face crumpled and tears fell for the millionth time today. "I couldn't find you!" I cried. "I woke up in wherever-the-hell-this-is and I was lost and I tried finding you and the will-'o-the-wisps took me here and that woman—"

To my utter surprise, he took me by the shoulders and hugged me to him, like I was some sort of treasure that he was afraid to let go. He wrapped his long arms around me and put his chin on top of my head.

"Sorry," he whispered. "I tried to find you as fast as I could."

I was so shocked by the sudden embrace, I stood stiff and unmoving. Then I melted into the safety of his arms and felt safe for the first time since I arrived here.

CHAPTER 10

"I THINK YOU MAY KNOW THE BEAN-NIGHE better as a banshee," Robin told me some time later, when my tears had stopped and we had set up a little fire for us to relax and warm up beside, before we started walking again. The mood between us had completely changed. Before, we had bickered and bantered. Now, though, it seemed like there was a wall that had come down between us.

"A banshee?" I asked, glad for the distraction from my empty stomach.

Robin sighed and sat back, the light from the fire that I had started, dancing across his face. "A woman who screams when someone dies. The Bean-Nighe in particular—" he pointed in the direction of the stream and I shuddered inwardly "—washes the clothes of someone who is about to pass on."

"So someone just died when I saw her?" I asked.

He shrugged. "Not too sure. They say that the Bean-Nighe is the spirit of a woman who died in childbirth."

I clasped my hands and felt my heart sink at the thought. "That's horrible," I whispered finally, "that she can't find peace even in death."

I thought about Alaina being pregnant with the baby that I was trying to find here. I hoped she'd be all right once everything was fixed. That there was nothing even remotely like this in her future.

"There are a lot of things that happen outside of our control," Robin said. "You have to make do with what you have."

Like being the only one in my family without magick.

"I wonder why the will-'o-the-wisps took me to her," I murmured softly.

A wicked smile came to Robin's features, exaggerated by the flickering firelight. "They were trying to help, I think. After all, her scream alerted me to where you were."

"What happened to you?"

He was silent for a long time before he scratched his ear and readjusted the position of his legs. I totally did not look at the flash of his abs or anything as he moved.

"I woke up in a nest of pixies that live as hedgehogs. I even landed on a few and had to pull out some quills." He grimaced at the reminder and rubbed at his back. "Luckily, Jack-in-Irons—the giant that we met—was nowhere to be found, so he must have kept going down the road. I wish I could have returned the favor and hit him back to the Winter Court."

His face took on a severe frown as he said that, so I felt like I should lighten the mood a bit.

"Thank you," I said softly. "For pushing me out of the way when the giant tried hitting me with that club." I gulped nervously. "I would have been killed."

He chuckled mirthlessly. "Well, you still owe me a favor, and you can't pay me back if you're dead."

So that was it. That was the only reason why he was here, a favor. I guess I shouldn't put any more stock into why he was here. I had to fight back my disappointment as I looked away.

"What kind of favor are you expecting from me?" I asked, dreading the answer.

He shrugged. "I don't know. Maybe your personality. Maybe your true love. Or…" He sidled up to me and met my gaze. "Maybe your youth and beauty. You have quite a few years left on you."

I gave him a horrified look, at which he cackled. Actually cackled.

"I'm kidding, Tinkerbell. Take a joke."

"Because it was *so* funny," I said sarcastically. Then I realized that he had said "beauty" and I tried to figure out if he meant that as part of his joke.

His eyes sparkled with mischievous humor. "I don't know," he said finally. "Don't worry, it won't be your firstborn child or anything. I don't want you going through Tir na nÓg again to get *that* baby, too."

I watched him, feeling my heart pound at his words and wondering what I should say after that. I settled on, "Good."

He chuckled and then fell silent, the reflection of the fire in his eyes. "Maybe my favor will be for you to take me out on a date."

Oh god, now my heart was in my throat. Did I really hear that right?

"What?"

He sat back, propping himself up on his arm. "Yeah, why not?" he asked. "I've been in the mortal realm for a long while now and these date-things are always fascinating to me. Sometimes there's more than the first date. Sometimes it doesn't work out. But, I'd like to see if it would work out."

"If going on a date works out?"

He shrugged. "If you and me would work out."

"Is that another joke?" I asked.

"What do you think?"

I looked at him, trying to figure if it was or not. A part of me, the part of me that was experiencing insta-love with him, wanted it to be so badly. Then again, another part of me freaked out at the thought, because the truth was, I *did* like him a lot. But he was a faerie, and I was mortal.

If that was all the favor would be, then I might be okay owing him more favors…

"So anyways, Tinkerbell," he said, his voice slightly ragged, "when all this is done, I—" He stopped abruptly and glanced back behind him.

"Aw, hell," he sighed, reminding me of what he said just before Jack-in-Irons showed up. That sent my mind into a panicked state of mind.

And for good reason, too.

I looked behind him to see a bunch of eyes watching us. Then a bunch of armored beings came out of the shadows, as tall as my waist. They were various shades of mossy green, with huge ears poking up from beneath their helmets. They were also chubby, big fellows with beer bellies that their tattered shirts didn't cover.

I could run from one, but there were at least two dozen watching us keenly. I had no hope of running, and I didn't trust my magick to get us out of this one.

"Goblins," Robin sneered, as much for my benefit as it was for him to hail the newcomers.

"Robin Goodfellow," the big fat goblin in the front hailed. "You're a wanted faerie."

Robin crossed his arms and rolled his eyes. "Everyone wants a piece of me."

He moved to block as much of me as possible from the lead goblin's sight. Like he was trying to protect me without bringing too much attention to it.

At least it seemed that way. Who knew what was going through his head?

"Queen Mab wants to see you," the big goblin said.

"I guess I'm flattered," Robin said, blinking in mock surprise, "that she'd send off the best of her goblin army to the Autumn Court to see me. You realize that this is trespassing, right? If anyone finds out, it could be an act of war between the Autumn and Winter Courts."

"A calculated risk," the goblin sniffed derisively, although Robin's words had the desired effect on the other goblins. They murmured amongst themselves, shifting their weight and looking very uncomfortable. Heck, I even felt uncomfortable myself at those consequences. I did *not* want to get caught up in a faerie war.

"Silence!" the lead goblin growled. "We won't get caught if everyone shuts up!"

That worked, and the rest of the goblins quieted. The leader peered around to make sure there weren't any stragglers before finally turning his attention back to Robin. "You're coming with us, Robin Goodfellow."

"Can't," Robin said in an offhanded way. "I already have a prior engagement."

That was when the leader tilted his head to look around Robin and saw me. Our gazes met and the goblin's face twisted into anger.

"A mortal?" he spat. "What is Robin Goodfellow doing with a human girl?"

Robin stiffened in front of me with a sharp inhale. He was trying to figure out how to get out of this one. At least I hoped so. I had the feeling that these goblins wouldn't take too kindly to a faerie traveling with a mortal girl.

"She's my prisoner," Robin said at last.

I blinked to make sure that I had heard that correctly.

"Prisoner?" I repeated at the same time as the leader. We both sounded incredulous, but for different reasons.

Robin grabbed my arm, and I hissed in pain as he hauled me to my feet. "Yes, my prisoner," Robin said. "I was actually just on my way to bring her to Queen Mab myself. You know, because I owe her Frozenness a favor."

"What are you doing?" I whispered, trying to figure out what was going through his head.

Robin flashed his eyes on me, cold, calculating, and warning me not to speak. This was completely unlike the Robin that I'd just been talking to a few minutes before. This was someone else entirely. Someone inhuman who I didn't recognize.

I shrunk under that cold gaze.

"She seems to think you're friends," the goblin grunted.

Robin shrugged. "All a part of the plan."

"But—" I protested.

"I know that Queen Mab likes mortal servants," Robin said, roughly shoving me into the space between us. I stumbled and fell, crying out in pain from my cracked ribs. "And since I've been, ah, indisposed and unable to come to the Queen's aide, I decided to do a make-good by bringing her a mortal girl." He glanced down at me. "This one has fire magick."

That got the goblins' attention. "Fire magick?"

"Yeah," Robin said, chuckling. "I tricked her into wishing for magick, and then brought her here. Isn't that typical of mortals to trust me?"

The goblins howled in laughter, like it was the funniest joke ever.

No, this was a trick that he was doing to protect me.

Although why, I had no idea. We just needed to get out of here and go to the Summer Court and everything would be fine.

His fingers dug into my arm, bruising the skin, and I had to blink wildly to keep my tears from falling. The betrayal, if that was what this was—even though I still had trouble believing it—hurt worse than the pain in the rest of my body.

"Robin, I—"

"She still thinks we're friends," Robin said, his eyes as cold as if we were already in the Winter Court. "But what can you expect from a stupid mortal?"

"Good one," the leader chuckled at the non-joke.

Suddenly they were all buddy-buddy, and I was at the center of their mocking.

After everything we'd been through together, I thought I could trust him. He had hugged me when I was terrified of the Bean-Nighe. He even called me Tinkerbell, for Pete's sake. Surely that wasn't all fake. Surely we were friends and this was a trick.

Surely.

"Stay back," I said. I staggered backwards. "The next person who touches me will feel the burn of my fire!"

To my despair, the goblins all burst into laughter, like I had just told the funniest joke. It wasn't meant to be funny. I'd been totally serious.

Even worse, Robin had joined in with their laughing.

"Oh, that's funny," Robin said. "Didn't I tell you

a long time ago that you couldn't do anything to me, Tinkerbell?"

He called me by my nickname, the name that I had started to like. That drove home that I was dealing with someone who wasn't who I thought he was.

He reached out and grabbed me. I screamed and unleashed a fury of fire through him. It was a stronger blast than the fireball that I had used to light up Jack-in-Irons's club. It should have set the faerie on fire.

Only, as soon as it hit Robin, it just fizzled out. Like it was nothing. Robin inhaled deeply and brushed off the one bit of his clothing that got singed.

"Well, she *had* fire magick," he said with a chuckle. "I guess she's used all of it up. Actually, I just took it."

I blinked in terror and sent another stream of fire his way. The only thing that I did was just wave at him. There wasn't even a bit of magick this time.

I started hyperventilating. Oh my god. What was wrong with me?

"She should be safe to handle now," Robin said, proud of himself. He gave me a toothy smile.

I whimpered despite myself as I was dragged between all of the goblins. They leered at me, binding my hands and my feet. I sobbed, terrified out of my mind, as they hefted me between all of them, like I was bodysurfing at some sort of horrible concert. Except that I was the center of attention of a horde of goblins.

"She smells like cucumber and melon."

"Her hair is blonder than Titania's!"

"Oh, look, she's crying!"

I heard a sobbing noise. Only then did I realize that it was me.

"We'll take her to Queen Mab," the leader said, somewhere out of my line of eyesight. I cried as one grabbed my hair and pulled me along.

"Nuh-uh," Robin's voice came. "Not without me. She's my present for the Queen, remember?"

"But of course," the leader chuckled. "She wants to see you too."

I couldn't see anything as I was pulled along. They carried me aloft above them, like I was on a palanquin of smelly, ugly goblins. It wasn't glamorous at all.

The goblins moved through the woods, fast enough for the trees to become blurs. I couldn't keep up with them and I gave up fighting, the pain from my ribs and my hunger taking over. So I just went along for the ride.

When Autumn gave way to Winter, I knew that I was more alone than I had believed possible.

CHAPTER 11

I DECIDED PRETTY QUICKLY THAT I HATED the Winter Court more than any other place in Tir na nÓg. It was freezing here, making my breath come out in little bursts of white and there was a serious lack of fae around. Having grown up in Jacksonville, where the coldest it ever got was forty degrees, I couldn't stop shivering. So while the goblins and everyone else seemed to be unaffected by the temperature, I was absolutely miserable.

Spent, hurt, and hungry, I let the goblins carry me. I wondered briefly if I was dying, because I had gone so long without food and water. Time seemed to move strangely in Tir na nÓg, so I blocked out the worry and focused on what was important: I imagined all of the various ways that I could punch Robin's face in.

I kept replaying every conversation through my head, wondering if it truly was all orchestrated to get me to Queen Mab. It would have been pretty elaborate, to gain my trust and take me to different courts. But something told me that faeries tricked mere mortals like me, and it wasn't out of the question.

I'd been had. If I ever got alone with him again, I

was going to set him on fire and watch him turn to dust.

In fact, fantasizing about it was the only thing that got me through our trip to the Winter Court. It's amazing how hate can both warm and freeze your core. It got me through the darkest part of the trek.

Eventually, the cold, open night and white fields started getting rockier and we started ascending a mountain covered in snow.

Robin didn't speak directly to me the entire time. Instead, he was up at the front of our little caravan, chatting away with the goblin leader like they were old buddies. Funny, because the leader had threatened Robin when they first showed up.

Oh, I hated them. I hated them all. If only my fire magick worked, I could get away from them. But then what would I do? Would I just hide out in Tir na nÓg for the rest of my days? Was there any hope of me rescuing Alaina's baby? Maybe I could go back and ask Titania if she'd take me as a servant again. At least there, I'd be treated better than anywhere else.

I shut my eyes and shook my head, unable to believe that I just thought that. Nothing about any of this was right. I had to find Alaina's baby and get out of here at any cost. If I had any chance of escape, I had to take it. Except the goblins kept a keen eye on me. For now, there was no way for me to get away.

Ugh, I hated faeries.

I spotted the castle ahead at the edge of a cliff. Like I

had pictured, it was a castle made entirely out of ice.

"How original," I muttered out loud.

None of the goblins acknowledged I had said anything, and Robin didn't even look back at me. That fueled my anger even more.

"Mab has done some renovating," Robin appraised, surprising me. Although not really, because I didn't care about anything he said.

"Yeah," the goblin leader agreed. "She had to do something after you melted half of it."

Robin chuckled lightly. "She should thank me. It looks much better this way."

I had no idea what it was before, but it was quite a sight now. Queen Mab apparently liked her castles tall and cold. While Titania's castle felt organic and made out of trees and flowers, the castle for the Winter Court was built like an impenetrable ice fortress. The structure rose as high as any skyscraper in Jacksonville, which was impressive considering that it was made out of ice.

I wish I had another joke to make of it. Then it wouldn't seem as imposing and terrifying.

I had nothing, except for betrayal and desolation.

As we came up to the entrance of the castle, I looked up to the see the tall, forty-foot high double doors in front of us. The Winter Court Queen apparently liked grand entrances.

My suspicions were confirmed as the twin doors opened and a lone, tall woman in black stood before us, her gown glittering like the night sky. Her dark, depthless ebony hair was bound up high on her head and her skin was as pale as the ice around her. Her eyes were an icy blue as she shrewdly looked at our little group.

"Robin Goodfellow," she said, and her cold voice sent a different kind of shiver down my spine. There was no emotion or really any personality in her voice. She was as cold as the frozen castle around her. "You have a lot of explaining to do."

To my chagrin, the red-headed faerie bowed deeply before the ice queen. "Oh your iciness, coldness, highness," he said. "I have only just been able to get back to Tir na nÓg to see you. I've been indisposed in the mortal realm."

Mab narrowed her eyes. "You still owe me a debt for what you did to my castle last time you were here."

"I am here to make amends."

Her jaw clenched. "There's a lot of amends you'd need to make for that."

So she still held a grudge against Robin. It seemed like this ice queen was unable to let it go.

Unfortunately, that caused Mab to train her icy gaze on me. Her eyes widened perceptibly as she strode towards me, the train of her black gown trailing through the snow.

"A mortal girl," she murmured. "How interesting."

"Yeah," I muttered. "Sure. That's what the last queen said."

"She's a present for you, my queen," Robin said without skipping a beat. He glared at me. "I know how you like playing with mortal lives."

Irritation twitched between Mab's immaculate eyebrows as she flicked her gaze back to him. "A present you say?"

"A first step as an apology for undoing all of the wrong that I've done."

Fury rose in my chest. "Robin!" I screamed, a flurry of curses on my tongue. "You no-good—"

I gagged as if my tongue went stiff in my mouth. Mab held her hand out, reminding me a bit of Darth Vader choking people with the Force. That's exactly what she was doing to me. Finally, she released me and I could breathe again.

Okay, so Mab was worse than Titania. Way worse.

The queen's lips quirked into a smile, and I didn't like that it was directed at me. There was something sinister in that smile that told me that I had to keep my mouth shut or else face her wrath.

"It's a fair start," the queen decided. "She should be interesting." She snapped her fingers. "Bring her to my receiving room," she commanded to the goblins. "I'd like to see who this girl is. And Robin—"

"Your Frozenness?"

"I want you there with me."

***

"ROBIN, WHERE HAVE YOU BEEN FOR THE PAST

few aeons?" Mab crooned from her throne.

It was a beautifully flawless room, with everything in it a variation of an ice sculpture or snow. Mab herself sat on a dais that made her seem imposing to all of her subjects. Granted, there weren't that many subjects in the room. While the Spring Court had been buzzing and vibrant with life, the Winter Court was a sterile environment. The only blemishes on the black and white color palette were the goblins, Robin, and me.

Mab fit right in with the world she created around herself with a palette of black and white.

I couldn't figure out how no one else froze like me. I kept shivering in the cold, and my skin was blue and covered in goosebumps. My fingers even had trouble moving because pinpricks of ice seemed to penetrate to the bone.

I was miserable, though no one else seemed to be.

"I was indisposed, your Frozenness," Robin said, stepping forward. I just wanted to wipe that smug expression off his face with a well-placed fire to his face.

Mab raised an eyebrow. "Indisposed, you say?" she asked, raising an eyebrow. "How? And—" she held up a finger in warning, "—do not call me 'your Frozenness' again or else I will make sure that you feel the extent of my powers."

I was too tired to feel smug at that.

"I have been in the Mortal Realm at King Oberon's request," Robin explained, his face going impassive.

Mab smirked. "Ah yes. Performing your lapdog duties."

The only indication that he didn't like being called a lapdog came in the form of him widening his eyes.

Then again, I could have just imagined it.

"You see," Robin continued, "King Oberon had a bogie desert his warm summer lands for...greener pastures, if you will."

"You're saying the bogie became a solitary fae?" Mab asked, taking an interest in his words.

"Indeed. And Oberon was heart-broken because it was his favorite bogie. Surely you've heard of Fiddlesticks the Bogie?"

"I have not, and I don't have much use for Oberon's play things. Including yourself, Robin." She snickered. "Foolish. Bogies never did have much of a brain between them. The Mortal Realm is a mess these days. It's suicide for faeries to go there."

"Agreed."

She stroked her chin in thought. "Funny you should bring up solitary fae though. I just had a bunch of pixies try to bargain for a place in my Court."

That perked up my ears.

"What did you say?" I whispered.

Robin shot me a look before turning back to the queen. "Pixies?" he asked.

She waved her hand away as if she was dismissing the thought. "Just a bunch of pixies who were desperate to earn their way back into our good graces. They had baby with them, can you believe that?"

"No!" Robin exclaimed in mock surprise, putting a hand to his mouth in a scandalous gesture. "You don't say!"

Hope fluttered to life in my chest. This was where Robin was going to look back at me and wink, giving me an insight that this was all a plan for him to get information out of Mab. That he wasn't really tricking me into being a mortal gift for this queen.

Except nothing ever goes how I want it to.

My hope died as he snickered back at me. "Funny you should say that about pixies and a baby, your Graceness. Our little mortal girl here is looking for a bunch of pixies and a baby."

Mab threw her head back and laughed, sending shivers down my spine. The Winter Court Queen laughing was not a pretty sound on the ears. It felt like nails on a chalkboard, and I gritted my teeth.

"What would she want with a bunch of pixies and a baby?"

Robin shrugged. "She thinks she can save the baby."

Ouch. Really, ouch. I bit back my tears and my retorts.

"Well, the mortal girl is entirely in the wrong Court," Mab said, wiping icicle tears from her eyes. "Apparently she and pixies have the same intelligence level. Pixies should know that they'd freeze in my Court after being here for some time." She waved her hand dismissively. "I sent them on their way to the Summer Court. After all, what use would I have had for a human baby?"

The Summer Court.

I had been on my way there, and if that giant hadn't gotten in the way, I'd have been able to appear before King Oberon and gotten Alaina's baby back. Maybe that could have spared me from Robin's betrayal. I wouldn't have gotten to this point. Heck, I'd probably be home right now, snuggled up under my covers, glad to be out of this mess.

I didn't notice that Mab had moved from her throne. She descended, every step making ice crystals spread around her. The very air itself grew colder as she came right up to me.

"But I do have a use for a mortal girl," she murmured softly. She reached out and grabbed my chin, roughly inspecting me. "You could be useful against those ingrates Titania and Oberon. A bargaining chip."

What was it with faeries and bargains? "I'm not a bargaining chip," I muttered.

She smirked and turned away from me. "I can imagine Titania wanting this girl in her Court," she told Robin, completely ignoring me.

He grinned wickedly. "She already offered. And Abby turned her down."

Mab quirked an eyebrow. "Oh, really? I'm sure that went over well. Titania never could handle rejection."

"No, she couldn't. Plus, the girl has fire magick, so you know that Titania was jonesing for it." Robin crossed his arms as he watched me.

That was it. My last trump card. I had hoped that I had one last secret here so that I could escape. Then again, where would I go if I did get out of here? Robin's face was unreadable, and I twisted my head away from him. The betrayal between us was too great.

"Oh?" Mab asked, as she turned back to me. "Fire magick, you say? That's a little dangerous in a Court made of ice and snow."

"You better believe it," I spat.

Mab turned back to Robin. "She's a little hostile, isn't she?"

"Like all mortals," Robin agreed. "Don't worry, I've got her magick on a tight leash. I told her it wouldn't work on me. But…you know how humans are…"

"She tried turning it on you, didn't she?" Mab asked. She clapped her hands, taking delight in my futile attempts to escape.

"Yeah," Robin said. "Yeah."

"So why are you offering her up to me, then?" Mab asked. "You're Oberon's pawn. You're kind of siding with his enemy, aren't you?"

Robin's jaw tensed slightly before he shrugged off her comment. "I got tired of looking for that bogie. Life gets boring when you work for the same people. So I came to try to bury the hatchet, as they say."

At the mention of the conflict between them, Mab's eyes flashed angrily. "Yes, although it will take a lot to forgive you for what you did to my palace last time."

Robin indicated the room we were in. "You certainly had a good architect to make it look much better."

Her lips pressed into a fine line. "Quite."

I picked up his cheeky insult to her old palace too. I was just too tired to point it out. After all, what good would it do? I was already screwed anyway.

At the thought of how tired I felt, I swayed on my feet, unable to contain it anymore. The movement caused Mab to glance back at me curiously.

"Apparently my mortal girl is feeling tired," she mused.

She called me hers. I would've been sick again if I had anything left in my stomach. Her eyes glittered as she watched my exhaustion and pain, as if she could look directly through me and see that I was nearing the end of anything keeping me together. I was too tired to speak, too tired to stand.

Too tired to be anything remotely human, to be honest.

"Knobhead! Where's Knobhead?" she barked, and the leader goblin shuffled into position.

"Here, your grace," he said.

Her gaze fell on him and a slow smile came to her lips. "Why don't you take my little mortal girl to the menagerie? She'll fit in well between the selkie and kelpie. There's a space for her there, isn't there?"

I had no idea what those two things were, but surely they were better than the queen in front of me.

"Sounds good," I muttered through dry lips. Then I gave Robin as hard and angry of a look as I could muster and said, "Any company is better than Robin."

The bastard didn't even shrink under my gaze. Instead he quirked a smile and patted me on the shoulder. "I'm sure you'll fit right in there. Remember, I've got a leash on your magick, so don't try anything."

If I had the energy, I'd definitely try something, but it was gone, so I just nodded as Knobhead the goblin took my bound hands to lead me out of the throne room. I almost felt relief, even though Knobhead's hands were warty and covered in a cold slime.

At least I was getting out of here.

"Hope Winter is your favorite season!" Mab shouted behind me shrilly. Then she laughed like she had said the funniest joke ever and the host of goblins joined in with her.

Robin didn't though. Instead he just gave me satisfied nod and turned away.

Oh, I owed him a favor all right.

A swift kick in the nuts.

CHAPTER 12

I WOKE UP SOMETIME LATER THAT NIGHT, although it was always night in the Winter Court, so it could have been two hours later or three days. Based on how stiff my muscles and joints were, it had at least been a considerable nap. My fingers were still blue and goosebumps covered my bare arms, but I had stopped shivering at some point during my sleep.

I don't know if that was a good or a bad thing.

There was an ethereal light in the dungeon—excuse me, *menagerie*—making a sort of eternal blue twilight to allow me to see the world around me.

I was completely alone in my cell that was about eight by eight feet across. Each wall was the same, semi-transparent ice. After waking up, I forgot which side was the door, because they all looked the same. Being semi-transparent, however, was slightly terrifying as I had no privacy, and I still had no idea what kind of beings the selkie and the kelpie were. I saw their shapes move across the frosted glass-like surface of the walls, but I couldn't make out the finer details and it wasn't like we could communicate with each other.

Yet, if they were prisoners in here like me, then maybe we had a shared goal of getting out. We were already allies, even if they were the kinds of faeries who might want to eat me.

I still had no idea how I was going to get out of there. I was too weak to really move, and if anyone offered me up a bucket of KFC chicken from a location in Tir na nÓg, I'd eat the whole thing no problem, consequences be damned. If I was stuck here, at least I'd have a full belly.

I combed my fingers through my hair, wincing as the strands got stuck. I hadn't showered in too long. Hadn't eaten since that pork casserole forever ago. My throat was parched and dried. And my ribs ached from being kicked by the giant.

Was this where it would all end for me? I should have been planning for my prom in a few weeks. Or looking into colleges. Or watching YouTube clips. I *used* to be normal. Then I wished it all away and traded it for this.

I failed everyone who counted on me. Jordyn, Mom, Alaina.

And worse, her baby. It was stuck in Tir na nÓg with me

I had no idea what kind of a future a human baby would have here. Would it be raised as a faerie? Maybe it would change and grow wings and become a king of its own seasonal court. I imagined Oberon letting it grow into a knight and marrying it off to a fairy princess.

No. Fairy tales were stupid, I decided.

With haphazard fingers, I wiped away tears from my eyes before they froze on my cheeks. Was there nothing here that didn't make a person miserable? Even the simple act of crying was torturous.

I leaned against the wall, watching the dark shape of the kelpie or the selkie move on the other side. As if it sensed me watching it, the shape stopped and then got darker as I saw the outline of something on the wall.

With trembling fingers, I pressed my hand to the spot. We stayed there like that, two rebels in solidarity.

Maybe, just maybe, I could use my magick and melt this wall.

I pushed my power into it, willing it to heat up. Not just for my sake, but for the creature on the other side. If I could summon up enough strength, it was a simple matter of melting this whole palace down around us, and we were scot free.

I'd figure out how to get to the Summer Court and get the baby after. The selkie and the kelpie, and all of the other creatures that Mab had stashed away, would be free. I would find a way back to the human world and put all of this behind me.

Except, my magick didn't come to me. Whatever stranglehold Robin had on it kept me unable to access my powers here. I gritted my teeth, flopped back to turn away from the shape on the other side of the wall.

"I'm sorry," I whispered hoarsely. "I can't help you guys."

On the other side of the room, I saw another dark shape move away from the wall, as if that creature had been trying to take part in our little moment. What good that did. All it did was disappoint me to the point of despair.

I leaned back and looked up at the ceiling, wishing I could see the night sky, even if it was different than the sky back home. To me, the night sky represented freedom, hope.

The boundless opportunities that life presented.

"If I could just see the night sky," I whispered, closing my eyes. I tried to imagine the sky that hung over Tir na nÓg, even the little snippets. "I just want to see the sky one more time…"

"Well if that's all you want, then…"

I froze, and I don't mean literally. I popped one eye open, afraid of who I'd see. Afraid of what I'd do if I did see him again.

Robin was crouching over me. In my cell. Like he was about to ask me for directions. I clenched my jaw, the rising anger in my body warming up my cheeks, and I sucked in air to spew as much bile at him as possible.

He held up both hands and shushed me. "I know, I know," he whispered. "You can hate me all you want, but I did it to save your life."

Incredulity edged its way into my vision. Amazing how I felt exhausted beyond comprehension before. Now I was ready to tear out his throat.

"Save my life?" I croaked, somewhere between a

scream and a sob. "You betrayed me! You sold me out to the ice queen!"

His face fell. "I had to do it," he whispered. "I had to make them believe that this was real for you. And I couldn't tell you that I was trying to trick them or you wouldn't have been genuinely mad at me. You have to understand that, Tinkerbell."

"Don't call me that," I growled. "How did you get in here, anyways?"

"I'm a faerie and I'm on Mab's good side. I can go where I please in her castle. At least for right now."

"I hate you. You betrayed me."

He swallowed and nodded. "Fair enough," he conceded, "but I had to do it. Back in the Autumn Court, the goblins had us surrounded. You would have tried to use your fire and they would have killed you because you are a mortal. And I would have lost you…"

The way he said that sounded intimate, romantic even, but I knew that wasn't the case. "Selling a person out to Queen Mab is the quickest way to lose someone."

"She would have killed you if she thought you were a threat."

"I would have been more of a threat if you hadn't taken my magick away!"

"I had to because I knew you'd get yourself killed. Mab is strong and she has no mercy."

"So kind of you to care," I said through gritted teeth

He combed a hand through his hair, mussing it up.

I wished he looked worse for wear, because I certainly felt papery thin at the moment. "I'm so sorry. I had to do what I could to make them not kill you."

I narrowed my eyes. "And all that about planning it from the beginning?"

Sad mischief danced in his eyes. "I'm a trickster, but I'm not that good of a trickster. I promise. You can even ask King Oberon when you see him. I've screwed up royally in the past."

I scoffed. "Kinda hard to see him when I'm stuck in an ice dungeon."

"Not for much longer."

Robin reached out to touch my cheek. I recoiled, trying to get out of reach, and he stopped.

"Abby," he whispered, "I'm trying to help you."

I didn't say anything, the fight drained from me as he touched my cheek. Surprisingly, his hand was warm, almost hot to the touch, and my skin warmed up where we connected. Despite myself, I closed my eyes and leaned into his hand, trying to soak up as much warmth as possible. I'd do anything for heat at that moment.

"Try now," he whispered, hoarsely. Suddenly, he looked as tired as I felt.

I glared at him. "That was all it took for you to restore my fire magick?" I asked.

He nodded slowly.

"I hate you."

"I know. And it's well-deserved too, but, hey, at least

you'll get out of here."

Maybe.

"I have to get myself out of here? I thought you had complete freedom here. Can't you just whisk me away?"

He sighed tiredly. "That's not how my magick works."

Faeries!

Fine. I focused the energy into my hand and funneled it in the fingertips. *C'mon, c'mon, c'mon.* For a few, long agonizing seconds, nothing happened. Panic edged into my brain and I thought he was trying to trick me again, to make more of a fool out of me.

Robin, it seemed, was full of surprises. His fingers linked with the fingers on my other hand, giving me more warmth, fueling the fire that burned inside me. I could now feel that fire deep inside me. It had just been masked, hiding.

But I had it now.

My hand jumped as a spark ignited in my palm. The ember glowed, giving me more life, like I had just caught my thirty-fourth wind. I released Robin's hand and cupped it around the fire. I gently blew into it, making it grow.

That was all I needed to get out of here.

I looked to Robin, who looked haggard in the firelight.

"I don't quite know your reasons for everything," I told him, my voice stronger now. It made me bolder than I've ever been before. "I'm not sure that I believe what you said about all of this to trick them. But I do want to get off this forsaken island, and I want that baby with me."

He nodded, spent. "Fair enough," he repeated.

That would have to do as far as reconciliation. I took the fire in my hands and used it to make my hands glow with the heat, almost like they were made out of molten lava. I pressed both of them to the floor and felt the ice give way to water.

Oh yeah. We were in business. My magick was new to me, but I could use it to melt this whole palace if I wanted.

I looked up and felt my own wicked grin spread across my features.

"Now we're talking."

***

MELTING PART OF THE FLOOR IN MY CELL created a chain reaction. Once I melted one part, it was easier to melt another part, and so on. I dissolved the door and went out into the corridor. Robin kept running towards the halls, but I skidded to a halt as soon as I saw the other creatures in Mab's menagerie.

"I'm going to let them out," I told him, nodding to the horse-like shape behind one door and the seal-like one on the other side of my cell. There were other creatures, all different shapes and sizes, and they were all prisoners of Mab.

"*These* creatures?" Robin asked, his voice in near hysterics. "But, Tinkerbell, they're—"

"Don't call me that!" I yelled at him. "And you can be as cowardly as you like, but I'm going to do the right thing for once."

Lord knows I haven't done anything right in a while.

I rubbed my hands together and pushed as much heat as possible into them. All I needed was a palm print into each one of the doors, and the chain reaction from melting would continue to melt the entire thing.

This was what I had to do. This was going to save a bunch of faeries who didn't deserve to be here. I just hoped they appreciated being saved more than they hated mortals. There were twenty cells that made up Mab's menagerie, and it took me a few minutes to imbue some fire magick into each of their doors. The water spread, warming the ice around it as it went down the hallway. The ceiling started dripping water, meaning that this was going to be a far bigger disaster than just destroying Mab's menagerie.

Creatures of all shapes and sizes came out of their cells, some dwarfing me, others barely the size of my index finger. One such faerie bent into a curtsey to thank me, before flitting out of the room.

"It's a brownie," Robin muttered. "Trying to win brownie points." He put his hands on his hips as a faerie that resembled a leg with a mouth and a single eye in the thigh hopped away. "I guess it helps to create a distraction for our escape."

"We don't need too much of a distraction," I muttered, finally seeing the giant horse-like creature walk out of its cell. I don't know much about horses, but it was taller than any Clydesdales I'd ever seen. Possibly bigger than any horse had a right to be, because its shoulder was at least a foot taller than me. It was all black with a straggly mane and red eyes that would have spelled a warning in any other circumstance.

But I felt an affinity with this creature. This was the creature that I had shared a moment with back in my cell. We both knew the odds. We both knew where we had to go.

I walked up to it and put my hand on its muzzle. "We'll just ride this horse out of here."

Robin's eyes boggled in his eye sockets. At least I could still freak him out. "*Ride* that thing?" he stammered. "Tinkerbell, that's a kelpie. It'll drag us down to the water, drown us, and *then* eat us."

The kelpie snorted derisively and shook its head.

"Oh, great," Robin exclaimed. "The kelpie is communicating with us."

The horse snorted in his direction, obviously not happy.

"Maybe it will take me to the Summer Court," I said.

At that, the horse nodded gruffly with a sniff.

"I'll take that as a yes," I said.

I grabbed the kelpie's mane as the big beast bent over. Despite the aching in my cracked ribs, I managed to pull myself mostly onto its back. The last bit of help came from Robin pushing on my rear, which made my cheeks warm from embarrassment.

At the very last moment, the faerie pulled himself up behind me.

"I'm coming with you," he told me. At my expression, he added grimly, "Whether you like it or not."

I glared at him, but finally nodded. Maybe I could sell him out to Oberon for something, and he could see how it felt.

The kelpie whinnied, not very happy that the other faerie was on his back. Like everyone else here, there was apparently bad blood between Robin and the kelpie. No time to settle that now.

"Come on," I whispered to the horse. "Let's show Mab what she's been keeping locked up."

The kelpie took off at a fast gallop, and, having only lived in Centerburg my entire life, without access to horses, I just held on for dear life.

The kelpie's hooves thudded down the hallway, and I watched as denizens of the Winter Court dodged out of the way. I was riding one of the most feared faeries in the Winter Court apparently. The rush it gave me brought a smile to my face, the first real one I'd had in a very long time.

The menagerie was on the ground floor of the place, tucked into the mountainside. Being dragged to my cell had taken a good thirty minutes. Riding on the kelpie, however, the halls and corridors flew by like I was flipping through pages of a book.

The other creatures of the menagerie ran alongside us, some leaping out to attack the faeries of the Winter Court. We neared the throne room on our way out, and I prepared myself for coming face to face with Mab. The kelpie didn't slow down one bit and we burst through the doors, the horse neighing wildly as it thrashed and kicked aside a goblin.

We had caught Queen Mab on her throne, and her look of horror, as we burst in with a bunch of wild and frightening creatures, was priceless. In a fit of inspiration, I held out one hand to her and extended my middle finger, igniting the end of it with a little flame.

She shrieked in anger.

I was triumphant and high on my adrenaline. The kelpie turned and streaked out of the throne room, through the doors, and into the night.

Just as I had wished for back in my cell, I got to see the night sky once again.

This time, I was sure it wouldn't be my last.

CHAPTER 13

IF YOU EVER HAVE TO TRAVEL THROUGH TIR na nÓg, I highly recommend doing it from the back of a kelpie. What took us hours before, now passed by in minutes, as the strong horse pumped its legs to cross as much land as possible in the least amount of time.

I held onto its mane and Robin held onto my hips as we rode through the different courts. Like in the Winter Court palace, faeries dodged out of the way as quick as they could to get away from the kelpie. I even spotted the knees of Jack-in-Irons at one point, but we were traveling too fast and too far away for it to be a problem.

Small miracles.

When we passed by any body of water, I could feel Robin tense up behind me, as if he was afraid that the kelpie would suddenly decide to take a dive with us on its back and drown us. I didn't worry though. The kelpie didn't seem to slow down one bit near water.

Eventually, Winter gave way to Autumn, which gave away to Summer, and the heat of the summer sun began to warm up my insides. It would probably take a long time for me to ever feel warm again after my stint in the Winter

Court, but I sighed, relishing the sensation of finally feeling my extremities.

I would never again complain about how hot it got in Florida. Heat was wonderful. Cold was its own kind of hell.

The grass here was green and lush, and the summer flowers were in full bloom. We passed by faeries that lounged in the sunlight, only giving us a cursory glance as we passed. Summer made you lazy with happiness. I know I sure felt that way.

The kelpie slowed down through the Summer Court, as if sensing that it was nearing our destination. I patted its neck, thanking it with every fiber of my being. I don't know if we would have been able to escape without it, and I certainly wouldn't have made it this far.

"There it is," Robin said, speaking up for the first time since he hopped on the back of the kelpie. It took me a moment to realize what he was talking about. I looked where he nodded and I saw the yellow castle rising out from the tops of the trees.

"The Summer Court," I whispered.

Summer and Winter couldn't have been more opposite to each other. While the Winter Castle had been made out of ice and snow and immaculately carved, the Summer Castle was simpler, with spires that wound their way up to the sky, reminding me of sunbeams. The walls were rounded, and the architecture reminded me vaguely of some Russian castles that I had once seen in a book.

Exhilaration hit me in the best and worst way possible. The best in that there was a strong possibility that the pixies and the baby were here and my journey was nearly over. And the worst way possible because, on some weird level, I was going to miss this place.

I must be crazy!

As we neared it, the kelpie whinnied again and stopped completely.

"This is our stop," Robin said, swinging one leg over and sliding down the kelpie's flank. His voice didn't hold the happy-go-lucky tone that it once had. In fact, he seemed melancholy and tired.

I leaned forward and kissed the kelpie on the back of its neck.

"Thank you," I whispered. "You saved my life."

The kelpie pinned its ear back in answer.

I hugged the horse around its neck and sniffled, trying to not let my tears fall. While we had a short time together, I would never forget what it did for me.

Sadly, I allowed myself to slide off the kelpie's neck. Robin caught me by my waist and gently set me down. I tensed my jaw as I looked at him, but I didn't acknowledge the gesture.

Only a little bit longer now and we'd never see each other again. Never mind that thinking that a while ago would have made me sad. He had revealed his true nature as a faerie. Now it was my turn to reveal my true nature as someone who could forgive, but not forget.

I brushed his hands away from me, refusing to allow him to touch me any more than was necessary. He frowned but didn't say anything more.

The kelpie neighed once more, filling the little valley with the sound, turned on its back hooves and galloped away.

"Who'd have thought that a kelpie would have been such a nice guy?" Robin murmured.

"It wants what any creature wants," I told him.

"What's that?"

"Freedom."

The space between his eyebrows tightened as he frowned down at me. "Listen, Tinkerbell—"

"Don't call me that."

"Okay, *Abby*," he sighed, exasperated. "I just…" His voice trailed off, and he swallowed back his words.

"What?" I asked.

He let out a breath. "I just wanted to say that I'm sorry for everything I've done. For any pain or hurt that I've caused."

An apology. It wouldn't right the wrongs that he did, but I found myself appreciating the gesture.

He grinned, seeing that his words had melted my icy exterior towards him. He held out a hand. "Friends?"

I hesitated for a moment before taking it. "Friends."

He then grabbed me and wrapped me up in a hug that wasn't tight enough to hurt my ribs. He put his chin on top of my head and breathed in deeply. The act had caught me by surprise, so I stood there, stunned for a few moments before stepping back.

"You tricked me again," I said.

"It's in my nature." He shrugged and the playfulness was back between us. At least we had that. "So you're not too mad for me to call in my favor after this, right? A date?"

I pressed my lips together, but I couldn't help the smile that was threatening to break across my face. "Maybe."

We walked up to the front of the castle gates, two imposing structures with patterns etched into the sandstone. In a way, it felt like we were looking at a giant sandcastle you'd find at the beach, which, in some ways, was entirely fitting for the Summer Court. However, unlike the other two castles that we've visited, the doors did not immediately open and no one came out to greet us.

"Hello?" I called out.

Nothing.

Robin crossed his arms as he tapped his foot. "I'm King Oberon's lapdog," he muttered. "You'd think he'd roll out the red carpet for me."

I chuckled lightly. At his raised eyebrow, I said, "You just called yourself a lapdog."

"So I did." He frowned again at the door. "Well, if no one is going to answer it, I guess we just help ourselves."

I was about to ask what he meant by that, when he reared his leg back and kicked the double gates open. The loud thud resounded throughout the meadow and the huge doors swung inward. No human could have done that by themselves.

I finally got a glimpse into what made him such a powerful faerie.

My wonder didn't last long, however, because as soon as the doors opened wide enough for us to see into the Summer Court Castle, I could see that all of the faeries in the Court were here to witness a shouting match between what looked to be a gorgeous Adonis of a man in his late twenties and Queen Titania.

Something hovered above them, like a reddish magenta marble the size of a bowling ball that glowed with an ethereal light. I looked at it, horrified.

Because cocooned inside the orb, protected from the elements, was Alaina's baby.

CHAPTER 14

TITANIA'S ATTENTION DIVERTED TO ME FIRST. As soon as she did though, her already angry face twisted into a nasty snarl.

"Well if it isn't Robin Goodfellow and the little hussy that turned down my offer for a spot in my court. How can this day get any better?"

The gorgeous, golden god blinked confusedly at us. "Robin?" he asked. "What are you doing here? And with a mortal girl?"

"King Oberon," Robin said. "I came with a mortal girl because she was searching for something."

Again, his whole demeanor changed as he addressed his king. For the first time, I saw just how much he had acted the part of the humble servant in the other courts. The faerie dropped into a low bow. This time, his allegiance was genuine.

Titania looked sick as she leered at him. "He came to trick all of us."

"Titania, hush," King Oberon said. "You will not speak to my servant that way."

Oberon turned, giving us his full attention. "Why

would you help a mortal girl?" he asked, sounding genuinely interested in what his servant had to say.

Robin sighed, and clenched and unclenched his jaw for what seemed like an eternity. Then he finally said, "Because I love her."

I blinked as the words sunk in. What the—?

Was this another trick? What the heck was he talking about? I swallowed the lump back in my throat as I tried to search his face. To my utter irritation, he refused to look in my direction to confirm or deny it. I wanted to shout in anger at him. This was cruel. He shouldn't be saying things like that, because something made my heart beat faster at the thought. And it wasn't right, because even though I felt insta-love, you don't go spouting things like that.

Right?

King Oberon laughed in his face. "A faerie? Fallen in love with a mortal girl?" he bellowed.

Robin smiled serenely. "It happened quickly as it does with faeries, but you know how fickle we are." He looked at me, his eyes shining. "It's just a phase, Tinkerbell. Probably. Maybe not. I at least want a date, but, it's okay if I also love you, right?"

I think if the ground opened up and swallowed me, I wouldn't have been more surprised.

He really didn't betray me at the Winter Court; he was trying to protect me. My heart fluttered to life in my chest, that maybe this thing I was feeling was actually being reciprocated. Yet now that we're here, at the end of our journey…

As if sensing my thoughts, Robin laughed shortly, and Oberon joined with him, but the laugh was mirthless, as if there was no conviction behind it.

"You always were a funny one, Robin," Oberon said with a smile. He looked at me fully now, taking in the sight of me, and I'm sure I looked like I'd just crawled out from the depths of hell, because this entire trip had pretty much been that.

Behind him, Titania was fuming. "I *knew* you had feelings for this…*girl* back at my court…" she raged.

I looked at her in a different light, as things started to click into place in my mind. With all of her disdain for Robin, it suddenly made sense as to why she'd want to keep me in her court; to get back at him in a petty way by taking something he cared about.

I really didn't like her.

Titania took it one step further and shouted, "And she should be thrown into jail for what she did to me!"

"I already have been, your highness," I said tiredly. "Back at the Winter Court. I really don't want to go back there again."

Oberon blinked and chuckled. "She's a funny one too, Robin," he said, as if I wasn't here. "I can see the attraction."

Robin gave me a sidelong glance, and his face was yet again unreadable. "Yes," he said simply.

"What is it that you are looking for, mortal child?"

Oberon asked, bringing my attention back to him.

I cleared my throat, forcing back my thoughts about Robin, and getting to the task at hand. Where should I start? Everything seemed like a blur right now, an adventure that came about in both dreams and nightmares.

I supposed I should start at the beginning.

I stepped forward, trying to ignore the fact that Alaina's baby hung deep in slumber above us. I was so close to my goal, yet so far. I had to choose my words carefully. I had to make sure that I would set this right.

"I made a wish within a Faerie Ring. Someone had tried to warn me—" I glanced as Robin as I said this "—but I was...stupid, as a friend once told me."

Robin snorted at that.

"Some pixies within the faerie ring granted it for me," I continued, "but it required a sacrifice, one that wasn't mine to give."

Oberon stroked his beard as he looked at me. "That sounds very familiar," he conceded.

"It is," I said. I pointed at the magenta orb of the baby floating in space above the room, like a trophy to be won. "That baby is my friend's unborn child."

The Court erupted into pandemonium at my accusation. Maybe I should have been more tactful with revealing that, but I couldn't stand there another moment while I was so. damn. close.

A swirl of tiny faeries flew to Oberon, too many for me to count, but their piteous, tiny cries sounded familiar to me. I clenched my hands, threatening to send a fireball their way and incinerate them. It was the pixies who had granted my wish and took the baby in the first place, and if they were here then…

"SILENCE!" Oberon thundered. His voice quieted the entire court. The pixies in front of him stopped chattering and hovered in the space between them. "We will discuss this like civilized folk!"

I glanced at Titania, who was looking at me with something akin to fascination. She hadn't been shouting. She just watched me curiously throughout it all. A slow smile came to her features and I was reminded that she was worse in many ways compared to Mab.

"See, my lovely ex-husband," Titania said. "You were trying to win me back by giving me a stolen child." As she spoke, her tone became more and more dangerous.

Oberon's jaw clenched. "Is this true?" he asked the pixies.

His question sent them in another flurry as they all tried to explain to him what happened. I couldn't understand them, but I could tell based on the other faeries' expressions in the court that they were making sense.

"They say that you offered up the child when you were granted your magick," Oberon said. "That they wouldn't be able to grant you a wish if it hadn't been offered to you in the first place."

Amazing that he could get that out of forty tiny little voices. I was impressed. I shook my head. "No," I said.

"That's not what I meant. Not at all."

Oberon sighed, and shook his head. "That's the problem with mortal conventions of bargains. You think you understand our rules when you really don't. You see, I had just accepted these pixies' offer of a mortal child for refuge within my own court."

"And he's trying to give the baby to me," Titania sniffled. "It's going to take much more than just presents to win me back."

"A baby isn't a present!" I yelled, my outburst surprising even me. "A baby is meant to be home with its family. To be loved."

Oh, my god, that sounded familiar. I saw a lot of myself in that scenario. Now I felt really homesick for Jordyn, Mom, and even Aunt Margaret. This had to work. It *had* to.

"I'm sorry," Oberon said, "but I've already made a trade with the pixies." He glared at Titania. "Even though Titania doesn't want it."

"You could feed it to the Nuckelavee," Titania offered. "At least it would offer some sort of entertainment."

"No," I whispered. Again, I had no idea what a Nucklelavee was, but I wasn't about to risk the baby to find out.

Titania grinned down at me, taking delight in my fear. "Or perhaps, the Hags of the Autumn Court would like to take care of it."

"Titania," Oberon warned. "You have not left my

court with the baby yet, therefore, it is still mine to give."

Still his…

"Wait," I said, hearing my voice waver as I spoke. "Faeries like to bargain, right? What if I traded you something for the baby?"

"Tinkerbell…" Robin hissed behind me.

I ignored him as I kept going. "Would you be interested in a trade?"

Oberon looked at me, considering my offer. "What would you be willing to trade?" he asked.

"You can't do that," Titania tittered. "You were just offering the baby to me!"

"And you hadn't accepted yet," Oberon pointed out.

"Then I accept," she said quickly. She'd do anything so I wouldn't get my way, the bitch.

Oberon gave her a grin. "We have a counter offer, my love."

My eyes flicked to Titania, who shot daggers at me with her eyes. I tried thinking through everything I had for trade. What would a faerie want? Here they were trading favors for unborn babies. While I trade magick for—

Oh.

That was it.

"I'll trade you back my fire magick." I licked my lips and looked at Titania. "Your grace would probably like that. Since I humiliated you earlier." She gasped in anger, but I kept going before I lost my nerve. "I traded the baby for magick in the first place. I will trade that power to get the baby and go back to my realm."

"Tinkerbell," Robin said quietly.

I ignored him, holding my breath as I looked at Oberon for an answer.

"You'd do that?" the king asked.

"In a heartbeat," I whispered. "You'd get the better end of the deal. It took the power of forty faeries to do it in the first place. You can have all that power to yourself."

The king fell silent for a few moments. Without a word, he reached out and touched my forehead and closed his eyes. I closed my own, screaming at him with my mind for him to accept the offer.

"I can't," Oberon said. He withdrew his hand and turned away. "Sure you traded for magick, but I need to get something bigger and better than that. You think you're powerful, but you're really not. And I have a chance to win back Titania."

No. I couldn't believe it. *No!* This wasn't happening. My heart sank as my jaw dropped. This couldn't be the end of it. My entire body went numb as this new reality set in.

I failed.

Titania looked smug as she smirked down at me. "Looks like you're not getting your way," she said. "Looks like it's not a happily ever after for you," her smile widened, "and Robin."

No.

This wasn't happening. Not when I was so close.

"Please," I begged, reaching out for Oberon. Water

filled my eyes and I couldn't see straight. "Please!"

"Your highness!" a voice shouted behind me. "If I may offer a counter offer to the counter offer!"

The king looked back and blinked confusedly. "Robin?" he asked. "What would you offer?"

I looked back at the red-headed faerie. His eyes were warmly on me as he smiled. There was a tinge of sadness to it. What was he doing?

Without taking his eyes off me, he said, "I offer up my magick as well."

Rather than the court erupting into pandemonium, the entire place stayed silent as everyone there thought about his offer. Even Titania's jaw dropped.

Without skipping a beat, Robin stepped in front of me, and bowed deeply to his king again. "So that's two bits of powerful magick for the price of one baby, your royalness," he said, falling back into the Puck that I knew so well. "You'd be a fool to pass that up, and—sorry, Tinkerbell—I have to say that my magick is much more powerful than yours. That means it's worth more. And that also means," he grinned at the king, "that it's a very good deal now."

"You'd offer your magick up?" Oberon asked in disbelief.

Robin nodded playfully. "Yeah. Although I warn you, it does come with some baggage."

"You can't do this, Robin," I told him. "What are you—?"

"Take it or leave it, your majesty," Robin bellowed, cutting me off. "I have the feeling that there's a baby that needs to go back home. Into some lady's womb."

"You realize that you are mostly magick by this point," Oberon said. "You're one of the oldest living creatures in Tir na nÓg. Without your magick, you may become nothing. There may be nothing left for you to exist on this plane."

"I'm fully aware of that, your Royal Crownness."

"Robin," I pleaded, "you can't—"

The king chuckled sadly. "Is it that awful being my servant?"

Robin nodded gravely. "The worst."

The king smiled, a real genuine smile this time. "Then I guess I have no choice, but to accept the bargain."

"No!" I shouted. I ran up to Robin, took his hand, and pleaded with him. "You can't do this! Robin, why are you doing this?"

"Because I can," he said simply.

"But *why*?"

He blinked, taken aback. "I thought I already made that clear. *Multiple* times. I. Am. In. Love. With. You."

"If that's true," I rasped, "then you can't do this. Please? What about our date?" *Because I think I have feelings for you.*

He chuckled and looked down at me. "I guess I may not be able to go on that date," he said softly. "So let me call in that favor now." He stroked my cheek as he said that.

"I want you to let me do this for you. So that you can save you friend's baby and go home."

My "no" died in my throat as his lips pressed against mine. A kiss. A wonderful, sublime kiss from the faerie that had been helping me through thick and thin. The faerie that had saved my life. The faerie that was giving up everything because of my failure.

I clung to him, willing a different outcome into this situation.

But it didn't come.

He broke the kiss and smiled down at me. "Now go back to being a normal human. And get something to eat, will you? Your stomach growling has been distracting this entire time."

Really? That was going to be the last thing he said to me? I opened my mouth to say more, but as I did so, the very fabric of the world tore around me, stretching me farther and farther away from Robin.

As I was swept away, I cried out…until I was lost to the darkness.

CHAPTER 15

"ABBY? ABBY?"

"Ugh," I groaned through dry, chapped lips. I tried opening my eyes, but I grimaced as too much sunlight seeped its way in between my lids. Why is sunlight so bright?

"What are you doing out here?" the same voice asked me.

That was...*Jordyn's* voice?

A thousand different thoughts and sensations ran through my head, but the few that stood out to me were: *Where am I? Is the baby okay?* And, *Where's Robin? Did he survive the bargain?*

The last one made the hole in my heart ache. I had no way of knowing if he was all right too.

"What am I doing out here?" I repeated, dumbly.

Suddenly, it felt like real, coherent thought made its way back into my numb brain. I jolted awake and immediately winced as my cracked ribs screamed in pain. That certainly felt real.

"Whoa, easy there," Jordyn told me. She smiled and laughed, her pink hair catching the sunlight. "You must have slept wrong. How did you fall asleep on a bench anyways?"

A bench. I blinked and sat up, finally able to take in where I was. We were outside in the garden of the hospital. This was the last place I saw Robin before he whisked me away to Tir na nÓg. I'd gone down here when we went to visit Alaina after her baby was stolen. And now…

Now it was morning. Now my heart hurt in ways I couldn't quite comprehend just yet, and I could feel the empty ache in my chest that had always been there. My fire magick was gone. I was just a normal human girl once again.

Before, that thought would have made me sad, but right now, it meant that things were as they should be in my world. That was all I could ask for, wasn't it?

"How's Alaina?" I asked.

Jordyn sighed and sunk deeper onto the bench. At first, I couldn't tell if it was a happy or sad sigh. Then she turned her head over towards me and grinned widely.

"She's just fine," she said, relieved. "They ran another battery of tests on her this morning, and, I guess the machines they used to monitor her baby or something weren't working."

"Because?" I prompted.

She laughed and combed a hand through her hair. "Because the baby is there and it's fine. The doctor has no idea what happened. I mean, Alaina and James could sue, because, you know, that kind of malpractice could have sent Alaina into shock and…"

"So she's okay?" I breathed happily.

Jordyn chuckled. "Yeah, she's fine. Sorry I didn't find you until now. I just didn't want to leave Alaina's side like that."

"No, it's fine," I said. "I was just so exhausted and scared for her, that I think I went out here and passed out." A likely story, I guess, because Jordyn nodded her head in understanding.

"I'm so glad that worked out," she sighed. "You have no idea how devastated Alaina would have been if…if anything had happened."

I could hardly guess at that.

I reached over and hugged my big sister as tight as I could. I didn't want to let her go. We were totally different, but she was one thing I could always count on, even when I messed up.

I understood now. I understood why she'd do anything to do what she thought was right.

"Hey, what's that for?" she asked.

"Just missed you," I whispered. "Plus…I'm just so relieved about Alaina."

"Yeah. Me too."

"Can I see her?" I asked.

"Of course," Jordyn said.

Then, to my chagrin, my stomach growled, loudly.

"Actually," I admitted, "I think I need to eat first."

Jordyn laughed. "Mom's pork casserole was that bad,

huh?"

"Well, I did ralph it up last night."

I remember barfing it out on the side of the road to the hospital. During my time in Tír na nÓg, I would have given anything to have it again. And I couldn't wait to see Mom again.

Jordyn rose to her feet. "I think there was a cafeteria on the second floor somewhere. Would that work?"

"*Food* sounds wonderful," I sighed happily.

***

"HEY ALAINA."

Jordyn rapped lightly on the door, where her friend laid in her bed. To my immense relief, her hand was over her burgeoning stomach. The baby was safe. That was all that mattered, right? She'd just been talking to her boyfriend and he held her hand as they talked about things couples do.

The gorgeous woman looked at us and grinned tiredly. *Relieved* was the word that came to mind when I looked at her. Relieved and happy.

I thought about the Bean-Nighe. Alaina was going to live a long, happy life with her baby, and that faerie that I had seen in the Autumn Court was a far cry from her.

"Hey," Alaina said.

"Hey," Jordyn said. "How are you feeling?"

"Like I'm six months pregnant." Alaina eyes fell

on me. "Oh, hey Abby. Listen, I'm sorry for the scare. It means a lot that you came all this way."

"It's all good," I said truthfully. Really, I had so much more to be sorry for.

"They're going to investigate what went wrong," Alaina explained. She sighed. "Got the fright of my life last night."

"I can't even imagine," I agreed.

She grinned at me. "Everything looks fine," she said. "They're just going to keep me for observation for a little longer to make sure that everything truly is all right. It was…scary there for a second."

"Yeah," I said. "I know."

How do you apologize to someone for causing the biggest, worst scare of their life when you couldn't go into the reasons why?

The simple answer was, I couldn't. Not if I wanted to stay out of an insane asylum. I had to keep this to myself. I'd ended up doing the right thing in the end, but the cost was high. I didn't care about my own magick, even though it was the one thing that I had wanted my entire life. No, I was thinking about a certain red-headed faerie who made my heart go pitter-patter. Who may have made the ultimate sacrifice so I could return back to my world with the baby.

Was Oberon correct? Was Robin so old, that to give up his magick meant giving up his life?

Oh no.

I hiccupped, feeling my tears start afresh. Regardless,

Robin was gone, and I'd never be able to see him again.

"Excuse me," I said, dazedly. "I need to step outside for a second.

Jordyn gave me a quizzical look, but I ignored it as I ducked out of the room and sank into one of the waiting room seats. Now that I was finally alone, I let my tears out.

It kind of felt good.

EPILOGUE

THREE MONTHS LATER

> *"So good night unto you all*
> *Give me your hands if we be friends,*
> *And Robin shall restore amends."*

I closed my copy of *A Midsummer Night's Dream* and sighed, as I clutched it to my chest.

"Oh Robin," I muttered. "You suck at restoring amends."

It was my tenth time to read the play, and while I still looked at some cheat notes, I was beginning to fully understand Shakespeare in a way that I never had before. It really was a beautiful story, and after my whole adventure in Tír na nÓg, I knew that a lot of it was based in truth.

Especially when it came to one character.

I was in the waiting room of the hospital with Jordyn and a few of their friends from the mermaid troupe. We were all anxiously waiting for news of Alaina's baby. I couldn't wait to see her son's face in the real world this time.

Jordyn sat across from me, and she raised a quizzical

eyebrow as she nodded at the book.

"Is that for school?" she asked. "I've seen you read it a lot recently."

"Something like that."

I knew that I'd probably re-read it a few more times and watch it being performed. If this was all that I had left of Robin, then I was going to take it.

"That's one of my favorite Shakespeare plays," their friend, Tara, who wasn't much older than me, said. She just flew in yesterday from Texas to visit her family in Jacksonville and to be here for Alaina. Like Jordyn, she seemed like one of those too-cool people, and her smile came easily. "May I?"

I reluctantly handed my copy over to her, mainly because I didn't want to part with it. She took the book and flipped to one page. "'*The course of true love never did run smooth*'," she read out loud. It was like she knew exactly where to flip to in order to get me right in the feels.

It was so true too. I clenched my hands as I cast my eyes down. I hoped no one saw my sadness there. But Jordyn, being my big sister and probably because of her magic, saw my expression. I saw her frown, but she didn't say anything.

"I never did get around to reading that one," their other friend, Christine said. She was older than all of us, but she laughed and acted like she was our age. I liked her already.

"You should," I said, taking back my copy from Tara.

"It's a good one."

"I used to read Shakespeare," their boss, this old guy named Neptune, said. "Especially his sonnets."

Next to me, I saw Tara frown and I knew that there was more to his story than just him being a Shakespeare fan. Maybe a long-lost love? I had no idea.

I didn't have time to wonder. "It's a boy!"

We all turned to see James, Alaina's boyfriend, standing in the doorway, wearing a blue pair of scrubs. He looked both shell-shocked and full of wonder, as if life was everything it was supposed to be: a miracle. You couldn't wipe that smile off his face if you had the world's biggest eraser. And who would want to? His family was perfect.

In the three months since my time in Tir na nÓg, I never had any doubt about my own sacrifice to get their baby back. Maybe I doubted and wished that Robin hadn't done his part.

This made up for a lot of it.

We all stood up and congratulated him, patting him on the back, and telling him how great a father he's going to be. Both he and Alaina were going to make great parents, and I couldn't wait to meet the little guy.

"Can we see them?" I asked.

Everyone stopped, caught off-guard by my eagerness to see the baby.

"Of course," James says, slowly, "Alaina's tired, but…"

"Great!"

I pushed past them and practically sprinted to Alaina's room. I skidded past the hallway and hurried my way to Alaina's room. I flung open the door and stopped in the doorway because I was transfixed by the scene in front of me.

There was mama holding her baby like he was the most precious thing in the world.

He was.

Tiredly, Alaina looked up at me, but she couldn't hide the smile from her face.

"Abby," she said, surprised at my appearance. She recovered quickly and beckoned me with her head. "Come meet Lucas."

I peered down at the bundle she had in her arms. I haven't been around babies much, but this one was pink and new. His eyes were closed as he napped on her chest.

"Hey little guy," I said. *Remember me at all? The last time I saw you was in a faraway land.*

Actually, it was probably better if he didn't remember. Being kept in a marble by a bunch of pixies and all.

I waggled a finger at him and got the hugest smile on my face when he wrapped one tiny hand around it. Tiny hands, tiny fingers, tiny fingernails. He was a whole person in such a wonderful, perfect package. "He's perfect," I said to Alaina.

She beamed at me. "He is, isn't he?"

Our eyes met, and while I couldn't get the stupid grin off my face, we shared a moment. Alaina may never know it, but we shared a love for this little guy. After all, I had the adventure of a lifetime to get him.

"Oh my god, Alaina!"

We both turned to see Jordyn in the doorway, flanked by all of her mermaid coworkers, and behind them James and Luke peered into the room. Everyone had big dopey smiles on their faces. And why wouldn't they? This was one of the biggest moments of Alaina's and James's life.

Jordyn, Tara, and Christine surged forward and started talking all at once to Alaina, cooing over the baby. She introduced Lucas to them and their faces just melted as they talked to him.

Now I felt out of place. I got up from the edge of the bed and made my way to the door. I needed some air. For such a happy occasion, I felt indescribably sad. Mainly because this whole moment wouldn't have happened without the biggest sacrifice from a faerie that I used to know.

I swallowed back the lump and ducked out into the hallway, ready to make a dash for the garden outside. I wanted to be alone so I could cry by myself. I just needed to be alone.

I bumped into someone's solid chest.

"Oof!" I coughed at the unexpected body check. Whoever I ran into had been moving down the hallway at a fast clip as well, and he reached out to steady with me. Only, when I looked up, I saw a familiar face. One that I thought I'd never see again.

"*Robin?*" I gasped in disbelief.

The red hair was the same, the perfect angles of his cheek bones, the height, his lithe build—everything about him was the exactly the same. But there was something different about him, like that spark of *otherness* was gone. He was wearing a pair of scrubs, and while his name tag identified him as Nurse Robin, he seemed…*different*.

He frowned down at me, confusion twisting in those eyebrows of his. "Yeah," he said. His voice even sounded the same. "Do I know you?"

He didn't recognize me. My initial reaction was to feel hurt and disappointed, but I really couldn't feel that way, could I?

This was Robin, but he wasn't fae: he was *human*. No magick. No faerie mischief.

What happened to you?

He was a normal human, just like I was. Did that mean that this entire time, there was a human boy named Robin Goodfellow who didn't know that he shared a likeness with an ancient faerie, who gave up everything just so a mortal girl could finish her quest?

The implications of that made my jaw hit the floor. *This entire time…*

And he didn't remember me at all. Then again, how could he? This was an entirely different being. He probably had a family nearby, friends, a dog waiting for him at his apartment. Probably a girlfriend.

I licked my lips and tried to hold back my gush of

emotions.

This isn't the Robin you know. I had to accept that.

I smiled weakly and staggered backwards. I'd been fantasizing and wishing for Robin to come back to me, and here he was, just completely different. Fate had a weird way of messing with me.

I shouldn't tell him a single thing. I should let him live his life in peace. He deserved that after everything that had happened. After being a pawn for a faerie king and dealing with all of the rules and mischief of Tir na nÓg.

I owed him that much.

"I'm…sorry," I said with a laugh, trying to cover up my shock at this recent turn of events. "I thought you were someone else."

Like the old Robin I knew, he snorted in a laugh. "You called me by my name," he said. I forgot how much his voice made my insides twist in anticipation. "So you must have heard of me before."

Move on, Abby. I shook my head. "Really," I said, even though the word burned my throat. "I had mistaken you for someone else. Sorry."

To hide my shame, I turned and walked away down the hallway. I needed to get to the garden, take out my phone and listen to some angry Taylor Swift to get my mind off him.

I could feel his eyes on me as I went, every footstep harder than the last.

"Hey," he called after me suddenly. "Who did you

think I was?"

I glanced back at him and offered a small smile. "A villainous Peter Pan."

That was a crazy thing to say. He even let out a mystified chuckle as he thought about it. "A villainous Peter Pan?" he asked. "Well, that would make you Tinkerbell, wouldn't it?"

I froze at the nickname, trying not to let my shock show on my face, but I think the world swallowed me up and ate me whole. This wasn't real. This was too weird.

I masked my shock by twirling a strand of my blond hair through my fingers.

"Yeah," I said. "I guess that does make me Tinkerbell."

Leave this, Abby. Before you get your heart broken.

"Hey," Robin said. He stuffed his hands in his scrubs pockets, a gesture that reminded me so much of his faerie counterpart. "I know this sounds crazy, but…" He let out a breath and chuckled. "I'm off in ten minutes, and while the cafeteria here doesn't have anything great, maybe we could…have lunch together? I mean, I bumped into you, it's the least I can do to make up for scaring you like that."

I blinked at him, letting those words sink in.

"Are you asking me on a date?"

A lopsided grin came to his face. "Yeah," he said. "I guess I am, Tinkerbell."

Wonders never ceased. I didn't know what magick it was that brought us back together, but I found myself nodding in agreement.

"Okay," I agreed. "Lunch it is. So long as it isn't pork casserole."

I may not have believed in faeries before. But now, after everything, I believed in a possible happy ending, too.

ACKNOWLEDGEMENTS

AS ALWAYS, IT TAKES A VILLAGE TO WRITE A book, even a novella that feature characters that I've visited twice before. So many people go on this journey with me. I am honored to know each and every one of you.

To Blazing Indie Collective, you guys amaze me with your raw talent. I'm so glad to be able to say, "I know them!"

To Margo and Lateia, you were with me in the trenches for this book. I think we made it out alive.

To Emily and Lori, you two are my inspiration and my sanity.

To Lindsay, thanks for saving my butt. Many times.

To my Nerd Crew, I hope you like it. I wrote this for you.

To my friends and family, I love you guys.

To Chris, you're my rock.

To my readers, thank you for taking this journey with me.

The adventure continues for Christine in…

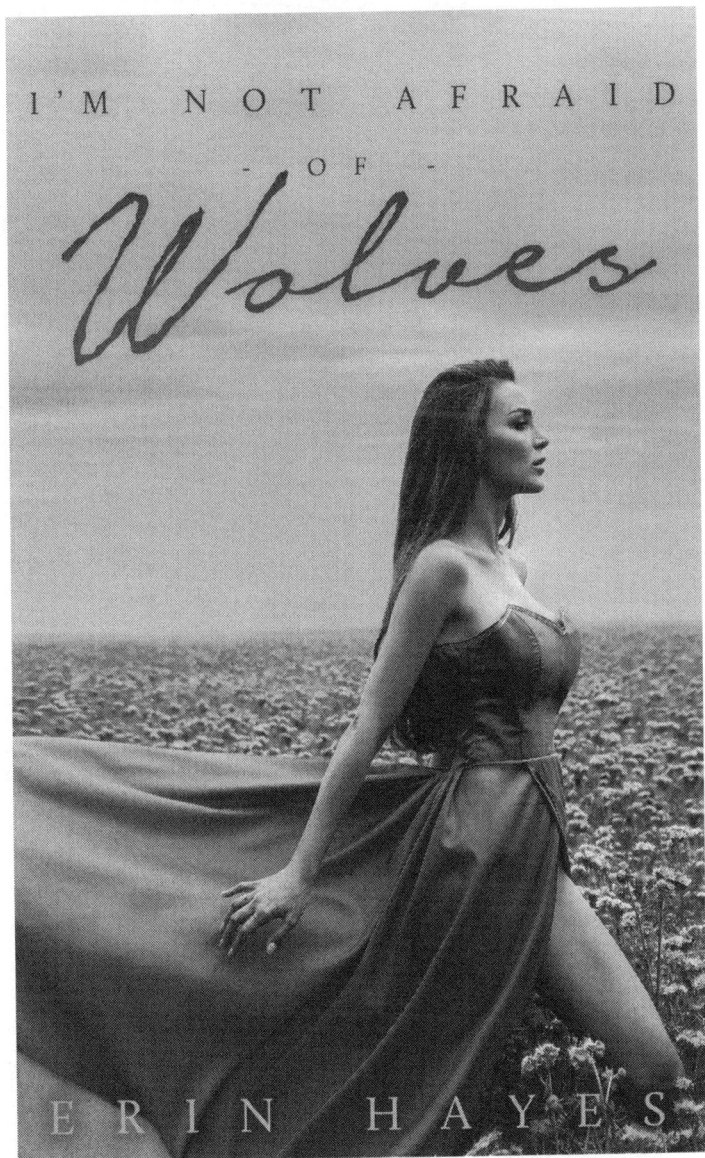

Coming in Summer 2016 as part of
the Blazing Indie Collection Monster Collection.

ABOUT THE AUTHOR

Sci-fi junkie, video game nerd, and wannabe manga artist Erin Hayes writes a lot of things. Sometimes she writes books.

She works as an advertising copywriter and moonlights as an author. She has lived in New Zealand, Texas, and now in Birmingham, Alabama with her husband, cat, and a growing collection of geek paraphernalia.

You can reach her at erinhayesbooks@gmail.com and she'll be happy to chat. Especially if you want to debate Star Wars.

Follow her on:

www.erinhayesbooks.com

www.facebook.com/erinhayesbooks

Join my street team at: http://www.facebook.com/groups/erinsnerdcrew/

Made in the USA
Middletown, DE
27 June 2016